Confessed

Vargas Cartel Series, Book 3

Lisa Cardiff

Confessed

Limitless Publishing, LLC
Kailua, HI 96734
www.limitlesspublishing.com

Formatting: Limitless Publishing

ISBN-13: 978-1-68058-303-8
ISBN-10: 1-68058-303-4

Dedication

To my sisters.

Chapter One

Hattie

My eyes fluttered open.

A maze of fuzzy shadows greeted me.

The pungent smell of ammonia flooded my senses.

My arms and legs prickled.

A film of humidity coated my skin.

My head throbbed in time with the rest of my body.

Hunger clawed at my stomach.

Thirst shredded my throat, making it nearly impossible to swallow.

I reached for my skull, and my arms shook with the effort. Metal shackles decorated my wrists like rusted bangles. Chains secured to the cement block wall dangled from metal rings on my shackles, clattering against the concrete floor every time I moved.

I traced my hairline with my fingers. Blood crusted on the side of my face and hair. My cheek felt puffy and sore to the touch.

I remembered fighting with that man on the street in Playa del Carmen. I remembered him striking the side of my head with his gun, but after that, everything was blurry like a fragmented nightmare. Non-distinct memories flashed through my mind like photographs.

A long car ride with a musty pillowcase over my head.

Arguments about where to take me.

Being pulled out of the car as my knees scraped across the dirt.

A phone call to Ryker.

Then, nothing…until now.

Keys rattled outside the metal door at the far side of the room. Seconds later, the deadbolt clicked, and the hinges squealed as the door sprung open. A fluorescent light overhead flickered to life with a slight hum. I squeezed my eyes closed, protecting them from the sudden burst of illumination. I heard the faint tapping of cockroaches scattering away from the light.

"*Buenas tardes,* Miss Covington." The gravelly voice echoed off the walls, and I pried my eyes open.

"Hello," I said, my voice scraping like sandpaper across my vocal cords.

"Do you remember me?"

I nodded, and pain shot through my head. "You're Juan Alvarez."

"Good." He flipped open a silver colored folding chair propped against the wall and settled into it, his ankle crossed over the opposite knee. His stomach hung over his wide black belt. "We had to sedate you, so I didn't know how much you'd recall from our first meeting."

My lips parted as images flitted through my brain one after another. Juan Alvarez had threatened to rip off my fingernails and deliver them to Ryker along with other body parts if he didn't return Anna Alvarez back to her family. Then, I lost it. I screamed. I kicked. I bit. I tore out his hair, and I ended up here—chained and caged like an animal.

My lips curved upward into something resembling a smile when I noticed the scratches carved into his cheek. I did that. I curled my hands into fists like a professional boxer. I narrowed my eyes into predator-like slits. If I weren't chained to the wall, I'd attack him again. "I remember enough."

"Right." He stroked the side of his face, then stood. He paced back and forth in front of me without saying a single word. Dirt crunched under the weight of his black loafers. The tassels on the tops of his shoes swung back and forth like a hypnotic pendulum.

Without warning, he stopped moving, and his hands threaded into my hair. He yanked my head backward, and it collided with a dull thud against the wall. I chomped on my lower lip to stifle a whimper. It fucking hurt. My brain scrambled, and the corners of my eyes stung with dehydrated tears, but I refused to cry. I refused to show weakness. It wouldn't help me. I'd melt into a blubbering puddle of fear, and I needed be coherent in order to survive.

"I don't tolerate disobedience. You try that shit again, and I'll fucking kill you. I don't give a shit who your family is or who your boyfriend is. You'll be nobody after I chop you into a million unrecognizable pieces and feed you to the coyotes. *¿Entiendes?*" His sour breath wafted across the side of my face, and I gagged. A lopsided smirk split his bloated face. The gold crown on his front tooth winked at me, taunting me.

I nodded, clenching my teeth to stop them from clacking together as full body tremors possessed me.

"Enrique," Juan spat as he glanced over his shoulder. "She's ready for you."

"Ready?" I whispered with my stare glued to the door.

A man with wavy dark hair that brushed the top of his shoulders strolled into the room. He wore faded baggy jeans and a black muscle shirt. Colorful tattoos of cartoon-inspired naked women and phrases in Spanish decorated his forearms. A bandage circled his right bicep. He couldn't have been more than five years older than me, but something about him scared the shit out of me.

"I'm looking forward to it," he said as his eyes traveled the length of my body. He pulled a cigar out of his pocket, snipped the end and lit it, his inky eyes never leaving mine.

"Enrique is my son. He's going to do the honors. I'm just here for the entertainment." Juan untangled his hand from my hair and sat back down in the folding chair. "I like having front row seats to these events. I find them inspirational."

My eyes widened, and I scooted backward, suctioning my spine to the wall. "No," I whispered, shaking my head back and forth. "No. I'm sorry. I won't do it again. I promise. I'll be good."

"It's too late for apologies," Enrique said. He sucked on the end of his cigar, and his cheeks hollowed, highlighting the knife-edged angles of his face. "But it won't be too bad this time. This is a warning. Next time…" He shrugged. "It'll be much worse."

He crouched in front of me, brushing the side of my jaw with his knuckles. "Such pretty skin. Not a single blemish. Personally, I like a woman with a few scars. They give you character. They tell a story about who you are and where you've been. When I'm done with you, you'll definitely have a story."

My heart battered against my chest bone, and a parade of uneven pants escaped my mouth. Like a thief, fear crept through my body coating my muscles in ice. I inched backward again, hoping and praying against all logic that the wall would open up and transport me anywhere but here. Where was a portal to another dimension when I needed it?

"Do you know what happened here?" He pointed to the bandage on his arm.

"No," I muttered, my voice almost inaudible. My words were thick and fuzzy.

He flicked his cigar, and the ashes landed on the neon yellow laces of my running shoes. The ashes glowed orange, then faded to gray dust a few seconds later. "I guess you wouldn't." He sucked his lower lip into his mouth and his spike silver labret piercing lurched forward like a snakehead. "Your boyfriend shot me as I watched that worthless piece of shit, Rever Vargas, drag my sister down the steps of our church. Can you imagine abducting someone from church?" He clicked his tongue against the roof of his mouth twice. "And here I thought the Vargases were all about honor and respect. Imagine my disappointment when I realized they're animals just like the rest of us."

My eyes widened as I stared at the bright white bandage. "I'm sorry. I didn't know," I whispered. Against all logic, I hoped it would make him reconsider his plans for me.

He tipped up my chin with two fingers and rubbed his calloused thumb across my lips. "Don't worry about me, sweetheart. I'll have a scar, but I'll be fine in no time."

He took another drag of his cigar and the sickly sweet smell of tobacco curled into my nose. Coughing, I turned my head to the side.

"So," he said, pushing my sleeve up my arm. "I've been thinking about how to get even with Ryker Vargas for shooting me and discipline you for your outburst this afternoon."

My stomach freefell like an elevator with its cables severed. "How?" I said. The word splintered as it rolled off my tongue.

He smiled, but it didn't reach his vacant eyes. "We'll have matching scars."

"No," I cried, yanking my arm away from him, but it didn't matter. He snatched it back easily enough. I couldn't escape.

He rolled his lit cigar between his index finger and his thumb for a suspended moment. Then, he grabbed my arm, imprisoning it against his thigh, and he plunged the glowing tip into my bicep.

I screamed as the cigar sizzled against my skin. Fire shot up my arm, and my muscles recoiled like a rubber band. The cloying smell of cigar mingled with the smell of seared flesh and burnt hair. My body jerked as shockwaves of pain radiated up and down my arm, echoing in my ears like a drumbeat.

"Please stop. No more," I begged as tears crawled down my cheeks.

"Oh, I'll stop." He pulled the cigar away from my arm and relit it with a flick of his silver lighter. "When I get bored of this."

My heart stuttered. "Oh my God. Please, no more."

I tugged my arm back, but Enrique stepped on the chain shackling me to the wall, and the rough metal edges of the cuff tore into my underside of my wrist. He dug his finger into my blistered wound. Curses tangled with screams flowed like a river from my mouth.

"Two more should be good unless your reactions disappoint me, in which case, I won't stop with your arm." He tilted his head to the side. "Now that I think about it, I do enjoy branding my victims." He brushed his fingertips down my arm. "Do you think Ryker would mind looking at an A while he fucks you?"

I whimpered and my vision slanted.

"How many places do you think I'll be able to brand you before your boyfriend delivers Anna back to us?"

Panic zipped through me. I squeezed my eyes closed, and my throat narrowed to a pinprick. "I won't move again. Just finish what you started."

He flicked his finger against the middle of my forehead. "No cheating, Miss Covington. You have to watch so you fully appreciate my artistry."

"No," I gasped, hooking my fingers in the hem of my shorts.

"Open your eyes or I will staple your eyelids to your eyebrows," he growled.

Spittle showered my scrunched up face. I bit the inside of my cheek, swallowing back all the insults I wanted to hurl at him. They wouldn't do anything except bring me more pain. "Go ahead," I said as I cracked my eyes open one by one. My mind floated as I circled through memory after memory, trying to hold on to anything to stop the pain and the anxiety as I waited for him to brand me again.

"Buena chica," he muttered, his voice dripping with ridicule as he pressed the cigar into my arm adjacent to the first mark.

Tears blurred my vision as I willed myself to stay still and keep my eyes open. Flames of agony rippled through my arm as my skin wilted like burning paper, curling up at the edges. My eyes locked on his. A smile twisted his lips into a sadistic sneer, and he lifted the cigar again. His black eyes glittered with a sick satisfaction as he lit it again and inhaled.

"Una vez más," he said as smoke exited his mouth in uneven puffs.

The cigar smashed against my arm once more. I didn't move. I didn't respond. Hate coursed through my veins, and I plotted my revenge. Disjointed thoughts tumbled through my mind, each one more warped than the last. I visualized carving the lines of his tattoos with a knife until a river of blood poured from his arms and neck. I mentally pierced his eyeballs, plucked them out of their sockets and stuffed them down his throat until his suffocated. I imagined his severed body parts scattered across the room.

I was deranged. My thoughts turned my stomach, but something about conjuring ways to torture and kill Enrique brought me clarity and purpose. It kept my mind from dwelling on the pain, and it gave me the incentive to keep fighting instead of succumbing to the defeat crushing my chest.

Then, it ended.

He removed the cigar from my arm for the fourth and hopefully final time. I sucked in a breath, filling my lungs with much-needed air. He caressed the side of my head, and I flinched. His touch made my stomach roll.

"Don't touch me," I hissed through my teeth even though I knew I should've kept my mouth shut and feigned compliance.

He sighed as he pinched my cheek, his dirty fingernails digging into my skin like two arrows. His putrid breath misted over my face. "Don't be tiresome. I can do whatever I want with you. You're our prisoner. You're mine until I decide otherwise."

I scoffed and ripped my gaze away from his penetrating stare. He could do what he wanted with me. I knew that, but it didn't mean I had to like it or acknowledge it.

Smiling faintly, he stood and tossed the cigar onto the floor. He ground the heel of his black boot into the fat stub. "That's all for today, but I'll be back tomorrow to finish the A. Two more should do it."

I glanced at my arm for the first time since he finished. Four circular burn marks marred my bicep, creating something that loosely resembled an upside down 'V'. I glared at him, wishing I could kill him with my hands instead of settling for killing and torturing him in my mind.

"Have a good night," he said as he turned to face the door.

"Wait. I have to go to the bathroom."

He didn't pause. He didn't stop. He pretended I didn't exist.

Juan Alvarez cleared his throat, and I focused my narrowed eyes on him.

"You can use that," he said, waving his hand at a small metal pail to my right.

A tremor rolled through my body. "What about food or water?" My throat was so dry I could barely swallow and my stomach was caving in on itself.

"I might have someone bring you food in the next hour or two if I remember." He flipped off the light and engaged the lock, bathing me in shadows again.

"Fuck you. I hope you burn in hell," I whispered.

Chapter Two

Ryker

"Good news," Ignacio said when I walked into his private hospital room twenty-four hours after I discovered Juan Alvarez had abducted Hattie.

"I find that hard to believe." I lifted my eyebrows as I settled into a chair on the far side of the room. To me, good news meant Juan Alvarez realized this whole thing was a big misunderstanding, and Hattie was waiting for me at the hotel.

Ignacio raised the top of his hospital bed into a seated position. "Don't look so defeated. My sons aren't losers or whiny pansies. Don't give up before we've started to fight back."

I exhaled hard out of my mouth. "Go ahead. Give me the good news." I hadn't slept last night. My mind flitted from one dead end to the next, trying to coordinate a rescue effort, but there was one big fucking problem. I had no idea where Juan Alvarez was hiding Hattie, and I didn't have the connections to figure it out.

To top off my problems, Rever wouldn't answer his phone or return my calls. If I couldn't get Hattie back in the next seventy-two hours, I would fly to Panama, hunt Anna, and drag her ass back here. Pregnant or not, I didn't give a shit. Hattie came first. Hattie was the only innocent party in this entire fucked up situation.

"Emanuel has narrowed down Hattie's location to two safe houses."

I leaned forward in my seat. Emanuel acted as Ignacio's right-hand man for at least ten years now, but he'd been affiliated with the Vargas Cartel for as long as I could remember. He'd systematically worked his way through ranks, and managed to ingratiate himself with Ignacio. In fact, he was the person who contacted me when Ignacio was shot over a week ago.

"How'd he manage that?"

Ignacio drummed his fingers on the metal safety rail on the side of his bed. "We have informants inside the Alvarez Cartel."

"So how long until he can pinpoint the exact location?" I didn't want to arrange simultaneous raids of two safe houses. Planning two raids would take time. A lot of time, and time was my enemy. I'd already wasted twenty-four hours. I only had two more days until Juan Alvarez made good on his threat to torture her unless he had already started, which wasn't altogether unlikely. Unlike in other criminal organizations, Mexican cartels didn't attribute any value to honesty. In fact, there weren't any rules except to show as much cruelty as possible in order to send clear and concise messages to your rivals. Mercy equaled weakness in the drug smuggling world.

"Two or three days. Maybe a week."

I shook my head. "That won't work. I need the information today or tomorrow. I have to attack before the seventy-two hour deadline."

Ignacio snorted. "I've known Juan Alvarez for a long time and his deadline doesn't mean anything. I can't believe he actually mentioned one. If he plans to hurt her, a deadline won't stop him."

I swallowed over the sudden tightness lodged in my throat like a rock. He hadn't told me anything I didn't know, but having him utter the words out loud killed any lingering hopes I had about rescuing her before she suffered mentally or physically.

"Yeah." I rubbed my hand down the side of my face. I hadn't shaved in days, and the bristles were almost soft to the touch. "You're probably right, which means every minute counts. I can't wait a week or two to find her."

Ignacio lifted a lidded plastic cup of water and sipped from the curved accordion straw. "Are you sure you want to do this? You could fly home and continue your life. Forget about Hattie, the Vargas Cartel, and Mexico. No one would know and eventually no one would care. She'd be another statistic, and you'd be free."

My eyebrows snapped together. "What the hell is that supposed to mean? I would know. Hattie would know. I won't let her die." If Ignacio knew about the baby, I don't think he'd act so cavalier, but I wasn't ready to tell him or any other member of my family.

He shifted his weight in the bed. Sadness lined his face. "There's a real possibility Hattie is already dead or well on her way there."

I jumped out of the chair and yanked on the collar of my shirt. I felt like I was coming out of my skin. "She's not dead."

"If she's not dead, then she probably wishes she were."

"No." I slammed my hand on the rolling food tray next to his bed. His fork clattered to the floor. "Hattie's strong. She'll keep fighting. She won't give up."

"And that's what scares me. When we abducted Hattie, we toyed with her because that's what the Deverons wanted. If she were any other hostage, we would've used her, tortured her, and inevitably killed her. With her bitchy mouth, she wouldn't have made it three days much less three weeks."

"They need her as collateral."

"They don't *need* anything. There is always another option to get what you want."

"If they want Anna in one piece, they won't harm Hattie."

Ignacio sighed. "You haven't spent much time with me in the last ten years, but the cartels have changed. Sometimes their crimes and viciousness shock the hell out of me, and I thought I'd seen everything. I hate to tell you this, but I know how Juan thinks, and he believes Hattie and Anna are disposable."

Rage and fear collided in my chest. My hands shook. I stuffed them into my pockets as I walked to the window to get my emotions under control. I needed to be composed and clearheaded. Knee jerk reactions wouldn't save Hattie.

I leaned my forehead against the window. There wasn't a single cloud in the sky and the trees were stagnant, almost frozen in time. Cars packed the two-lane street. Horns honked, and music spilled from their open windows. People strolled along the sidewalk, talking, laughing, joking, and living their lives as if they didn't have a care in the world. In comparison to me, they probably didn't. As much as I hated everything about my life, I would spend a hundred lifetimes in hell to give Hattie and our baby the life they deserved. And if living in misery guarantied her happiness, I would do it without regret for the rest of my days.

"I know things have changed since the last time I dabbled in cartel business with you and Rever, but I won't abandon her." I spun around. "It's my fault she's in Mexico. I left her unprotected while I helped Rever. I should've brought her to the Vargas compound until it was time to catch our flight, but I didn't think the Alvarez Cartel knew about her. I thought they'd be focused on Rever and Anna, not Hattie or me." I tugged on the cuffs of my shirt. My gut burned like I'd drank too many shots of Tequila on an empty stomach. "I didn't fucking think."

"You're right. You didn't think." Ignacio angled his chin to the side. "Juan Alvarez isn't an amateur. Not by a long shot. He has informants too."

"Who the hell would tell that two-bit piece of shit anything? He's got two fucking shipping routes. He's not powerful. He doesn't have much influence beyond a couple of small towns in your territory."

"Loyalties shift and bend every day. Juan's smart. He's been in this business for over a decade. You have to assume your enemy knows everything you know or you'll be caught with your pants down."

"Nobody knew Hattie was with me except you, Emanuel, and Rever."

"Exactly. Rever probably told a couple of friends and Anna Alvarez." His face scrunched up when he said Anna's name. "That's as good as telling the whole goddamn world. You might as well have left a note with Hattie's picture and location on the church steps when you and Rever took her."

"What's wrong with telling Anna? She's not going to tell her family anything. She wanted to get the hell away from them."

Ignacio raised one eyebrow. "I don't believe that for one second. Anyone with the last name of Alvarez cannot be trusted. If you had consulted me, I would've told you to let her rot in hell. I don't know for sure, but I'd bet my half of my fortune that Anna's jerking Rever around. She won't marry him. Hell, I bet she can barely tolerate him."

My brows flattened. "How can you talk about her like that? She's carrying your grandchild." His words didn't jive with the father I knew. Family meant everything to Ignacio, and Anna would be part of his family any day now. Rever planned to marry her as soon as possible.

He snorted. "I'll believe it when I have the paternity test in my hands. From the little I know about Anna Alvarez, that kid she's carrying could belong to a half dozen men."

I shifted on my feet. "Rever was pretty confident it was his."

"Because Rever is a dumbass. He spent the majority of the last three or four months in prison or with you. The timing doesn't add up."

"He came back to Mexico for a while," I argued, even though I was starting to believe Ignacio had a point. This whole thing could've been a set-up and the Alvarez Cartel played Rever or Rever played me. The thought caused my stomach to knot with anger.

"It's possible. I know," Ignacio agreed, nodding his head. "Rever could be the father if she's pregnant, but like I said, Anna Alvarez isn't a blushing virgin by anyone's account and she's not above lying either. This could be one more game in the war between our cartels."

I pinched the bridge of my nose. "So what do you think I should do?"

"Don't involve Rever in any of your plans. He can't be trusted right now. His relationship with Anna is clouding his judgment."

"I need his help. He owes me, and he has Anna."

"You'll have to collect on that favor later. Right now, you have to assume anything you tell Rever will be fed to Juan Alvarez."

"You think so?"

"I know so," he countered.

Pacing the length of the hospital room, I weighed my dwindling options. Nothing was foolproof. Nothing would unwind the damage. Nothing would make Hattie whole.

I paused, sucking in a deep breath. "In that case, I think I'll call Rever and tell him I'm not going after Hattie. I'll tell him I'm going to report her disappearance to her family and the U.S. Embassy, and let them deal directly with Juan Alvarez."

Ignacio rubbed his hand along his jaw line, his dark eyes narrowed. "That's risky. They might decide she's not worth the hassle and kill her."

"I know, but they're probably expecting me to launch an attack any day. If they think I've changed my mind, they might lower their defenses, and I could catch them off guard."

"You might be right." Ignacio squinted his eyes as he stared over my head. "You need to get going. Emanuel is waiting for you at the compound. He wants to discuss a few things with you. Before you call Rever, ask him what he thinks."

I rubbed my hands along my thighs. "Do you think I can trust Emanuel?"

"Yes," he answered without hesitating. "He's the best man I have."

"Okay," I said as I walked to the door without a backward glance. Ignacio had told me to trust Emanuel more times than I could count, but something about him got under my skin.

"Call me tonight."

"I will."

Chapter Three

Hattie

"Are you hungry?"

I didn't move. I didn't open my eyes. My bones ached. My head hurt. I wanted to die.

"Hello?" Cold fingertips trailed across my forehead, and I flinched, anticipating more pain or torture. "Are you awake?"

"Leave me alone," I mumbled, but the words bled together. They sounded like a stream of incoherent grunts and moans.

"Sorry, I can't do that."

Lukewarm liquid dribbled across my lips, and I cracked my painfully dry eyes open. For a frozen second, I couldn't see anything. Black spots dotted my vision. I licked my lips, trying to draw every molecule of the unknown liquid into my parched mouth. My throat burned when I tried to swallow. I blinked my eyes, struggling to bring the person in front of me into focus.

"Who are you?" I croaked, staring at the gray-haired man hovering over me. Hard lines bracketed his eyes and mouth. His skin resembled a worn leather jacket. A sheen of sweat beaded at his hairline.

"The closest thing you're going to get to an ally while you're here," he whispered, his dark eyes unreadable.

Focusing on the cement block wall, I rolled to my side and pain ricocheted up my arm. *Crap.* I had forgotten about the cigar burns. Straining to move, I flattened my palms on the cold concrete floor and pushed my body upright, folding my legs to the side. Chains scraped against the concrete and the metal shackles bit into my wrists. "I don't have any allies here. Don't pretend otherwise."

He frowned. "You have a couple, but we can talk about that later. Right now you need to eat and drink."

My stomach rumbled as he placed a paper plate with some cut up fruit and rice on the floor next to me.

"What's your name?"

He cocked his head to the side as though he couldn't decide whether he wanted to tell me. He blew out a breath. "Raul."

I attempted to smile, but I strongly suspected it resembled a grimace. "Thanks for the food."

"It's not much, but it should hold you over for a while."

I nodded. "It's better than nothing. Can I have a fork?"

"No," he answered, shaking his head. "You might use it as a weapon."

"With these on?" I lifted my shackled arm and

flinched. "Fuck," I mumbled. It felt like Enrique had dipped my arm into the fires of hell.

He pursed his wiry lips. "Let me see your arm."

"It hurts to move it," I said as I stared at the angry puckered flesh on my bicep.

"This will help." He pulled a silver key out of his pocket and unlocked the shackle on my right wrist.

Red cuts encircled my wrist. I bent my wrist up and down and then in a circle. "Thanks."

"Eat. I have to put those back on soon. Juan or his son will stop by to check on you soon. They don't trust anyone."

I shoved a piece of watermelon into my mouth. The sweet juice burst in my mouth and coated my cracked lips. I hadn't eaten anything since I left the hotel room for a jog.

"What day is it? How long have I been here?" I asked as I grabbed a handful of white rice and shoved it in my face like an animal. If my mom were here, she'd be shaking her head.

"Thursday. You've been here almost two days."

"Do you think they'll let me go?"

Raul glanced over his shoulder.

"Or are they going to…" The words stuck in my throat. I wasn't ready to hear his answer.

He drummed his fingers on his thigh and his gaze flicked to the side. "I don't know. They haven't discussed their plans with me."

"Are you friends with Ryker?"

"No," he answered.

My brows scrunched together. "Then why are you being nice to me?"

He chuckled. "Money. Everything is always

about money. Don't you know that?"

"Who's paying you?"

"Here." He handed me an open bottle of water. "Drink this."

I drained the entire bottle, shaking the last few drops onto my tongue. I still felt dehydrated. I could've drank ten bottles. "Are you going to answer my question?"

"No. Are you done eating?"

I popped the last grape into my mouth. "Now I am."

"Good." He grabbed the empty paper plate and the plastic bottle. "Get some rest."

"As opposed to what? Doing jumping jacks while chained to the wall? Talking to myself? Watching the non-existent TV?"

He squeezed my chin between his thumb and index finger. "Listen," he growled. "Your friends and family might dismiss the way you talk to them, but the Alvarez Cartel won't and neither will I. If you want to get out of here alive, you need to shut your fucking mouth. This isn't a game. This is real. There are no second or third chances. They won't hesitate to carve you up into a hundred pieces and feed you to the animals."

Fear ghosted down my spine. "Okay. Okay," I whispered as I scooted backward. "I'm sorry. You're right. Can you tell me why I'm here?"

He sighed and rocked back on his heels. "You're here as collateral for Anna Alvarez. The Vargas Cartel took her so they took you."

"But I thought she wanted to go with Rever."

"It doesn't matter what she may or may not want.

Rever and Ryker humiliated Juan Alvarez and Ryker shot his son. If he didn't respond, he'd look weak. Looking weak won't do you any favors in the drug smuggling business."

"But what does any of that have to do with me? I don't have anything to do with the Vargas Cartel."

He shook his head as he wrapped the metal shackle around my wrist again. "Don't play dumb. We both know that's not true."

"Wait." I grabbed his arm. "Don't lock it. My wrist is killing me. If anyone comes in, I'll put it on."

He stood and wiped his hands on his pants. "Fine, but don't forget." He opened the door.

"Will I see you again?" Using the wall as support, I climbed to my feet. My vision blurred, and I swayed to the side like a drunken sailor.

He dragged a hand through his shaggy hair. "Maybe. Maybe not, but if everything goes as planned, you should be out of here soon."

"Soon? As in today?"

A faint smile spread across his face. "It's a secret. You don't need to know anything. Just keep your mouth closed and do what you're told when the time comes."

The door slammed and I slid down the wall, curling into a ball on the floor. Silently, I prayed I'd sleep until this nightmare ended.

***

"Wake the fuck up."

An open palm collided with my cheek and pain

vibrated from my chin to my temple. My eyes popped open. Enrique's nose was less than a foot from mine. His dark hair curtained the sides of his face. A sneer stretched his lips. My heart thumped in uneven intervals inside my chest. I scratched the side of my neck.

"I'm up. I'm up," I mumbled, slithering away from him on my back. The rough concrete scraped my bare shoulders.

He snatched my wrist, holding it less than an inch from my nose. "Who unlocked you?"

My eyes flared. "I don't know anything about it."

His hand tightened, strangling the blood flow to my fingers. "Don't lie." Spit showered my chest and neck.

"I don't know," I repeated. "I was sleeping. Maybe it fell off." I cringed as the words exited my mouth. No one would believe my metal cuff miraculously popped open, freeing me.

"Try again, Miss Covington." He twisted my arm to the side.

A scream erupted from my mouth and tears welled behind my eyes. *Fucking hell.* He was going to dislocate my shoulder.

"Okay. Okay. I stole the key. It fell out of Juan's pocket, and I kept it." I didn't want to tell him about the man who unlocked it. He said he'd help me. He couldn't do that if Enrique killed him.

He slammed my hand against the wall.

Once.

Twice.

Three times.

I yelled. I cursed. I fought, but none of it mattered. My entire arm blazed with pain, throbbing with every pulse of blood through my veins.

He stood up and kicked my thigh. "If you want to eat today or anytime in the near future, you need to start talking."

"I already ate," I groaned, rolling to my side, cradling my hand against my chest.

His eyes glittered. "Really?"

I nodded. "Yes," I rasped.

"That's the first interesting thing you've said all day."

My stomach somersaulted as his black boots stomped across the room and out the door. What the hell did I say? Why would it matter if I had eaten?

My lungs squeezed as the answer raced through my brain. No one was supposed to bring me food. No one was supposed to talk to me. A shiver danced down my spine.

I flopped onto my back, staring at the ceiling. I was fucked. I screwed everything up without thinking. Raul told me to keep my mouth shut and I failed.

"Do you recognize this man?" Enrique barked less than five minutes later.

I rolled my head to the side. Enrique dragged Raul into the room by his arm.

"I'm not sure." I dropped my gaze to the floor unable to meet Raul's eyes. "I don't feel so good. My mind is really fuzzy."

Enrique's leg shot out, connecting with the side of Raul's knee. Raul flew sideways and tumbled to the ground hip first. He rolled onto his side, clutching his left leg. Pain lined his already winkled face.

My stomach pitched, and bile climbed the walls of my throat, coating my tongue with acid.

"Oh my God," I whispered, through trembling lips.

Enrique yanked his gun from the holster at his waist and planted his black boot in the middle of Raul's chest. "I'll make this really simple. I'm going to shoot one of you," he said, his onyx eyes boring into me with the force of a laser.

My eyes bugged. "No," I begged as I scrambled to my feet. I staggered forward, trying to escape, but the chains jolted me backward like a retractable dog leash. "Please don't. Leave us alone. I didn't escape."

Enrique cackled like a hyena, and I had the urge to claw out his vacant eyes. "Ah, that's cute, Miss Covington, but whose life are you pleading for? Yours? Or his?"

"Both," I said immediately. "I'll put the shackle back on my arm and we can forget this whole thing." I grabbed the chain with my free hand, wrapping the metal cuff around my wrist. It squeezed my swollen, misshapen flesh. "I'm not going anywhere. No harm was done. Let's forget this happened."

Enrique waved the gun between Raul and me. "No. It's too late. What's done is done. Don't prolong the inevitable. You have a choice to make. Will you be a martyr or a murderer?"

"Neither." My legs were rooted to the floor.

"Wrong answer, Miss Covington. Try again."

Rolling his eyes, he tapped the barrel of his gun against his thigh. "Who will it be? You or him?"

My gaze collided with Raul's. I searched his face for a clue. His eyes darkened momentarily, then a mask of nothingness slipped into place.

"I don't have all fucking day. You have five seconds to decide, or I'll kill you both," he growled.

"Please, don't do this. Nobody needs to get hurt," I said, my body trembling like a leaf in a thunderstorm.

"Five."

The number bounced off the cement walls, and I bit the inside of my cheek until blood tainted my mouth.

"Four."

Air burst from my lungs.

"Three."

My vision swirled, and I closed my eyes so I didn't collapse on the floor. Enrique ensnared me in a nightmare, and I couldn't wake up.

"Two."

"Him," I screamed as my stomach plummeted.

Pop!

A gunshot exploded, ringing in my ears. My heart stopped for a frozen second. I couldn't move. I couldn't breathe. Time fractured.

"Good choice, Miss Covington," Enrique said. "I was starting to question your sanity."

I pried my eyes open. Raul's lifeless body was sprawled out on the floor. Inky blood spilled from a hole in the center of his forehead. Vacant eyes stared sightlessly at the ceiling. His lips were lax. Blood splattered the ground behind him like an experiment in modern art.

Sobs bubbled from my lips. I was a murderer. I chose my life over his. He wanted to help me, and I repaid him by ordering his death. I wanted to curl up and die. I deserved to die. I was evil. Ice crystals formed in my veins. I gagged and swallowed simultaneously, fighting back my nausea, but it didn't work. Chunks of the watermelon and white rice reversed course, spraying my sneakers.

"Why?" I cried as I wiped my mouth with the back of my hand. Tremors conquered my body one muscle at a time until my entire body shook.

"Because I didn't have a choice." He pulled a white cloth out of his back pocket and tossed it in my direction. "Have a good night, Miss Covington."

"Are you going to do something with his…?" My voice faded to silence, and I angled my head toward Raul's body.

"No. I thought you'd enjoy some company." He laughed. "I'll think of a way for you to show your gratitude later." Enrique turned and strutted out of the room, slamming and locking the door. I could hear him humming as he walked down the hall to whatever hell he came from.

I slid down the wall and covered my face. Guilt consumed me inch by inch, creating a crater-sized hole in my stomach. I couldn't look at Raul's lifeless eyes. I felt like I had an anchor attached to my ankle pulling into pool of quicksand. I was drowning.

Drowning in guilt.

Drowning in self-pity.

Drowning in pain.

Confessed

Drowning in heartache.
I didn't even know if I wanted to be saved.

Chapter Four

Ryker

"You think she's here?" I pointed at the pictures covering Ignacio's desk.

"I'm eighty percent certain that's where she's being held," Emanuel responded, lacing his fingers together on top of Ignacio's desk.

I snagged one of the pictures off the desk and studied the dilapidated, two-story, white stucco building. Black crisscrossed bars covered all of the windows. Twisting green vines crawled up the columns bracketing the faded wood front door. Glass blocks spaced every couple of feet circled the bottom of the first story of the home in a linear pattern, indicating the home had a cellar or a basement.

Seventy-two hours had passed since the Alvarez Cartel abducted Hattie. The deadline for returning Anna Alvarez had officially expired. Juan had threatened to dismember her part by part after the deadline, starting with her fingernails and moving on from there. Rage simmered in my gut at the thought. If he or any of his minions hurt her, I'd kill every last one of them and tear them to pieces with my bare hands.

"I need to know for sure. If we show up at this place and she's not there, they'll find out and kill her."

Emanuel licked his lower lip and looked away. "You're right, but this is all the information I've got right now, and I don't think I'll receive new intel any time soon."

I crumbled the picture and tossed it on the desk. "What happened to your informant? You said he'd know her exact location by now."

He rolled his shoulders. "I haven't heard from him in over a day."

"Is that normal?"

"No," he answered without elaborating. "But it's not entirely unexpected either."

I massaged the back of my neck. "Should we be worried?" Every hellish second that elapsed without seeing Hattie made the anxiety festering inside of me corkscrew tighter and tighter around my chest until I could barely take another breath.

"It's not a good sign."

"Meaning?"

"He's probably dead."

I ran my fingers through my hair. "Do you think Juan Alvarez knows he was working for us?"

He lifted and dropped one shoulder. "He knows we have informants inside his organization just like we know he has them inside the Vargas Cartel. It's irrelevant."

"What the hell's that supposed to mean?"

"In drug cartels, there is no such thing as loyalty. Money and power are the only things that matter. People are loyal to whoever pays them the most. Juan understands that. He expects it. We all do. Even Ignacio."

I leaned over, bracing my hands on the desk. "And what about you? Are you loyal? Or are you following wherever the money leads you?"

Emanuel brushed invisible lint from his shirt. "What are you trying to say? I've worked for your father since you were in diapers. I have done everything he's asked of me and more."

"What makes you different from the rest? Can Ignacio trust you? Can I trust you?"

His eyes hardened, then he waved his hand dismissively. "I'm different."

"How?" I snapped.

"Because I don't want anything else. I don't have a wife or kids, and I don't want them. I have more money than I'll spend in this lifetime. Ignacio values my opinion, and I don't have a target on my back like he does. I don't envy him, and I sure as hell don't want to be him or take his job."

"So if Ignacio died tomorrow, you wouldn't break out the champagne and designate yourself as the newest drug lord?"

He licked his lips. "No. I'd welcome Rever or you with open arms. Hopefully you, because we both know Rever wouldn't last a month. Everyone knows his weaknesses. Women. Gambling. Drugs." He waved his hand. "You, on the other hand, are a wildcard. Nobody would know what to expect, but anything is better than Rever. He's a disaster."

I studied him, searching for any signs of duplicity, but his face didn't reveal anything. My shoulders slumped. Either he was being honest or he had a first-rate poker face. "Fair enough."

Staring out the window, I turned my back to him. Shadows from the trees danced on the creamy marble floors. Terraced gardens filled with colorful flowers dotted the wall of green foliage. Was Hattie looking outside through a barred window in that white stucco prison waiting for me to come and find her? Had she given up on me or was she in too much pain to care? Did she hate me? Did she regret letting me back in her life?

I shook my head. I couldn't dwell on any of it. I had to rescue her and get her the hell away from Mexico and this shitty life. Everything happened for a reason. Maybe her kidnapping was the universe's way of telling me that Hattie and I weren't meant to be together. That we'd never be together. That we could never be a family. With or without the Vargas Cartel, I was a liability. One that Hattie and our baby didn't need or deserve.

"Okay," I said, whirling around to face Emanuel. "Let's plan this mission. I can't wait any longer. I don't know how long Hattie will last."

Emanuel nodded. "She could already be dead. You do realize that, right?"

My heart stuttered, and the pungent ache of guilt mixed with regret knotted my insides. "She's not," I said with more certainty than I felt at the moment. Images of Hattie's bruised and battered body drifted to the forefront of my mind.

I lifted the decanter from the desk and poured a

glass of whatever Ignacio had. I didn't give a shit. I needed alcohol to settle my nerves and take the edge off the anxiety flapping in my gut like a bunch of rabid bats.

I tossed back the entire glass of tequila in one swallow, forcing thoughts of Hattie from my mind. The liquid burned my throat, and my eyes watered.

"Tell me what you've planned so far," I said, slamming the glass on top of the desk.

Emanuel tipped up his chin, his eyes tight. "Pour me one of those, too."

My hands shook, and my pulse hammered against the base of my throat as I poured another glass of tequila. The liquid splashed over the rim onto a stack of papers. *Dammit.* I needed to get my emotions under control. Worrying about the future and things out of my control wouldn't save Hattie.

"Here," I slid the low-ball glass engraved with a V across the smooth desktop.

He nodded his thanks. "There's only one access point into this safe house. It's a one lane dirt road." Emanuel traced a faint brown line through the jungle on a satellite image of the house where he suspected Hattie was being held.

"I see that."

"According to our source, they have guards stationed at the base of the road and in front of the house, but no one along the sides or the back."

Squinting, I leaned forward. "So that's the weak spot. We'll attack from the rear."

"Or by the air."

My eyebrows crawled up my forehead. "No. Absolutely not. We'd announce our arrival. They'd kill Hattie by the time we landed. We need to hike through the jungle and approach from the rear." I tapped my finger on the aerial picture. "How far is this road from the safe house?"

Emanuel took a sip of his tequila. "A mile or two, maybe more."

"Then, we'll have our convoy drop us there and we'll hike up during the night."

"It's not an easy hike. There's no trail. It's straight uphill. Thick vegetation with lots of rocks. The guys will be too tired to fight by the time they reach the safe house."

"This isn't an easy job," I countered. "Hiking is better than having them shoot down our helicopter before we can get boots on the ground."

He spun his glass in circles on the table. Waves of tequila lapped over the side. "That all sounds good if this were a military operation. Not a lot of our guys are trained for a mission like this. We need people with experience and endurance."

"How many members have solid military or police training?"

"Members that are available on short notice?"

"Yes," I snapped, flexing my hands.

He cocked his head to the side. "Five. Maybe less. A lot of the members are former farmers or recovering drug addicts. I won't pull people from Ignacio's personal guard, and compromise his safety to rescue your girlfriend."

I shoved my hands in my pockets to stop myself from hurting him. "What about the Americans? Does Ignacio have any Americans on the payroll or people he's used on a contract basis in the past?"

He blinked a few times, then shook his head. "What are you talking about?"

"Don't play dumb," I sneered. "You know exactly what I'm talking about. Just like every other drug cartel, Ignacio uses US military veterans for special tasks. I'd like a few of them to join me."

I could call some freelance operatives I'd met over the last five years, but that would take time. Time I didn't have. I needed people who were already in Mexico and were familiar with the nuts and bolts of drug cartels. I didn't want to bring in some guy who usually worked with the Russians or the Jihadists. Every criminal entity had a different personality. Different priorities. Granted, greed and power were at the center of all criminal organizations regardless of whether they hid behind the veil of religious zeal, political ideology or flat out materialism. But I didn't want to waste time briefing someone on the intricacies of the Mexican drug cartels. I needed people already up to speed and familiar with the Vargas and Alvarez Cartels.

He leaned back in his chair, propping his hands behind his head. "He's used a few independent contractors hired on a job by job basis."

"Great. Hire them for this job."

His left eye twitched. "These things take time. I'll need a week to work out the details. Maybe more. It depends on their availability."

"We don't have a week. Double their standard rate. Make it worth their time."

Emanuel shifted in his seat, and our eyes locked. "I'll have to get Ignacio's approval."

"Then get it. I don't care about the money. I'll

pay the difference." I slammed my open palm on the table, knocking over my glass. It rolled onto the floor, exploding into tiny slivers as it collided with the tiles. "Offer whatever it takes to get the right people here."

He blew out a breath as he ran his hands through his hair. "Fine. I'll see what I can do. I know a couple guys who used to be in the Marines. They only take a few jobs a year. They might be compelled to accept this one if I tell them we're trying to rescue the daughter of a high profile politician."

"Don't reveal her identity until after they accept the job," I said.

His bushy brows knitted together. "Why not? We can use it in our favor."

"I don't want this incident to follow Hattie for the rest of her life. Being abducted by a drug cartel once is a tragedy. Two times would make her a circus sideshow."

"Why does it matter what people know? According to Ignacio, you're staying here to help him now, so she'll be here too."

A wave of guilt rippled through me as I poured another glass of tequila. "No. I'm putting her on the first plane back to the US. I'm done with her. I need to get her out of my life. She's a distraction I can't afford. Not anymore."

"All this for a woman you don't want anymore." The corners of his mouth curled up in a stomach-turning grin. "Interesting."

My lips flattened. I didn't care what Ignacio said about Emanuel. He rubbed me the wrong way.

Unfortunately, I still needed him, so I refrained from planting my fist in the dead center of his smug face.

"What the fuck is your point?" Hattie's absence in my life would be hard. I didn't need to explain myself to this asshole. She'd given me something nobody had. Unconditional love and acceptance, and now I had to throw it all back in her face. She wouldn't leave willingly. I'd have to break every promise I'd made to her and shatter her heart in the process.

He held up his hands in mock surrender even as his eyes glittered with anger. "Nothing. It's not my business."

"You're right. It's not." Against my better judgment, I downed another glass of tequila and grabbed the decanter. "When can we make our move?"

"Give me an hour to make some calls and if everything falls into place, we'll be ready to launch our attack in the next few days."

I opened the door to Ignacio's study. "Fine. I have some stuff to take care of. I'll be in touch later today."

I didn't wait for any answer. I was out of the house, stripped naked and diving into the pool less than five minutes later. I couldn't be around anyone right now. I needed to clear my mind and calm my nerves. I felt like a noose was tightening around my throat, and my sanity was dangling from a frayed rope.

Chapter Five

Hattie

Darkness and the stench of rotting flesh greeted me when I opened my eyes again. A damp draft kissed my skin. Scurries of rats or other vermin taunted my ears. Shuddering, I turned onto my side and my fingers trailed through a damp pool of what I assumed was blood. I gagged, but nothing came up, which was probably a testament to how hungry and thirsty I was.

I scrutinized the walls, the metal door, and the damp ceiling. Squinting, I could see the outline of Raul's body. I needed to get out of here. I couldn't wait for Ryker. It could take him weeks to find me and organize a rescue mission. Even then, he might not be successful, or I could be dead by the time he showed up. The events of the last couple of days demonstrated with blinding clarity that Juan Alvarez and his son wouldn't hesitate to kill me. If I hadn't told Enrique to shoot Raul, he would've shot both of us, and there'd be two rotting corpses on the floor right now instead of one.

I popped open the metal band around my wrist. I hadn't fully closed it earlier. I wiggled my fingers. My hand and arm still throbbed, but I could bend all of my fingers. Rolling onto my stomach, I army crawled through the pool of blood. It seeped through the front of my shirt and coated my knees, but I kept inching forward.

I needed to search his body for a weapon or a phone. I ignored the acid swirling in my stomach. I didn't want to touch his dead body, and I sure as hell didn't enjoy crawling through his blood, but I'd run out of alternatives. Raul intended to help me. Now that he was dead, I had to help myself. I needed to be strong. I needed to be smart. I had to take risks because cowering like a mindless drone wouldn't get me out of here.

My chains wrenched me backward like a bungee cord, and I couldn't move another inch. I stretched out my injured hand, trying to reach Raul. My fingers brushed across the hem of his pants. Tuning out the pain pulsing in my fingers, I curled my hands around his pants and yanked his leg. Pain shot up my arm, and I screamed, but I didn't let go. I gritted my teeth together and pulled as hard as I could.

When I'd moved his body a few inches, I wrapped one end of the dangling chain around his ankle and the other end around mine. Squeezing my eyes shut, I crab-walked backward, using my entire body to drag him closer to me. The chain bit into my skin with so much force I thought my ankle would split in half. Sweat beaded on my forehead. My muscles burned.

Finally, my back brushed against the cement wall, and my shoulders sagged in relief. I did it. Now, I could search his body.

I patted down one leg, then the other. I felt a lump around his ankle. I tugged up his pants and unstrapped a small pistol. Popping open the ammunition cylinder, I checked for bullets. It wasn't loaded.

Dammit.

I slid the pistol back into the holster.

Not wasting a second, I dove into the front pocket of his pants. I found a silver money clip filled with a quarter inch of folded bills. I leaned over his body and patted my hand on his other pocket. My fingers brushed against a rectangular object resembling a cell phone. My heartbeat rocketed inside my chest, echoing like a freight train in my head.

I fumbled, unable to find my way into his pocket. I inhaled through my nose to steady my nerves, and the smell of rotting flesh wafted into my nostrils.

"Oh my God. Oh my God. Oh my God," I mumbled repeatedly as I shoved my hand into the opening and snagged the object from his pocket.

A phone.

A freaking phone.

A thread of hope wrapped around my chest and a light laugh bubbled from my mouth. I swiped my finger across the screen. It only had twenty percent battery left so I had to move fast. With trembling fingers, I dialed Ryker's cell phone number, silently praying he'd answer his phone.

"Ryker Vargas," he said after the first ring.

"It's Hattie," I whispered, cupping my hand over the phone.

"Hattie, where are you?" His voice was clipped with urgency.

"I don't know. In some basement I think."

"Whose phone is this?"

"Raul's. He said he wanted to help me." I cleared my throat. "But he's dead. They shot him right in front of me."

"They shot him and left his body." It wasn't a question.

I nodded before remembering he couldn't see me. "Yes."

He didn't say a word for a few seconds. "Are you hurt?"

"I'm alive," I answered. I didn't want to catalog my injuries for him. We could do that if I ever got out of this place.

"I'm going to find you. I'm going to get you out of there. I promise. Just hold on another day and I'll be there."

I closed my eyes as relief flowed through my veins. Tears beaded like dewdrops of hope in the corners of my eyes. "Okay."

"What else can you tell me about where you are?"

"I'm chained to a cement wall. The room has a metal door and no windows." I glanced around the room, looking for any details I'd missed. A sliver of light peeped into the room above my head. "Wait, there are three glass blocks near the top of the wall. They're really dirty."

"What about the exterior of the building?"

"I haven't seen it. I woke up in this room, and they haven't let me go anywhere."

"That's okay." His voice dropped. "How much battery is left on the phone?"

I pulled the phone away from my ear. "Eighteen percent."

"Turn it off, but turn it back on tomorrow night and put the ringer on vibrate. I'll text you when I'm close."

"You know where I am?"

"I think so," he answered. A long drawn out sigh echoed like a faint breeze through the phone. "I'm sorry I let you down."

My insides twisted with regret, forgiveness, and anger at him and myself. I shook my head, willing all my conflicted feelings to disappear. "I should've stayed on the hotel grounds. I should've waited for you to come back."

"You didn't do anything wrong. I shouldn't have left you alone. I shouldn't have asked you to go back to Mexico with me." He cleared his throat. "I made so many mistakes."

Chills trickled down my back. "Maybe. Maybe not," I said because I couldn't ignore the truth in his declaration, but it didn't stop me from wanting him. Needing him. Loving him. He held my heart in his hands. He always would regardless of what he did.

I closed my eyes for a second to gather my thoughts. "Why did you do it?"

"What?"

"Help Rever." A sob erupted from my mouth. I gulped humid air into my lungs, trying to stop the torrent of sadness pounding on my chest. "Didn't you know you were putting us in danger?"

"I didn't think they knew about you." His breathing turned heavy, whistling through the phone in jagged pants. "And even if they did, I thought I could protect you. I thought I could outsmart them. I thought I could get us out of Mexico before they found you."

"Okay," I mumbled as I processed his answer. Anger pulsed through my veins, but it fizzled as fast as it materialized. As much as I wanted to hate him for failing to grasp the danger of the situation, the emotion seemed irrelevant when I could die tomorrow or five minutes from now. I didn't want to waste time hating him, punishing him, regretting him. Fate had already conspired against me enough times. I didn't need to give it another reason to kick me in the face.

"No matter what happens after this, remember I love you, Hattie. I always will," he said, interrupting the strained silence.

I bowed my head, resting it against the tops of my knees as I squeezed the phone like it was my one and only lifeline. I rubbed the budding ache in the center of my chest with the palm of my hand. This conversation felt awkward and wooden, and yet, I wanted to snag his words out of the air, and put them in my pocket forever.

I closed my eyes and summoned his image. In my mind, I traced the angular line of his jaw, down the strong column of his neck, following it over the smooth rise of his muscular chest and around to the thick bands of muscles bracketing his spine. I licked my lips as I recalled the salty taste of his skin. I inhaled, pretending his familiar scent filled my nose instead of the stench of death and despair. I missed him. I needed him.

"Yeah, I know. I believe you. I believe in us," I said.

Even though I denied him the reciprocal profession of love I thought he wanted to hear, it didn't stop the words from getting stuck on repeat, struggling to escape the confines of my mind.

I love you.

I'll always love you.

Forever.

The words simultaneously slaughtered and fortified my soul, but I didn't feel like I had the strength to console him or offer him forgiveness. We both had so many sins on our hands. We were broken, I realized with sudden clarity, and I didn't know how we'd fix it. I just knew we had to find a way.

"I'll see you soon, Hattie. Stay strong. Keep fighting."

"Okay, I will. Bye, Ryker," I murmured almost soundlessly.

I powered off the phone and hid it in the zippered pocket of my running shorts. I didn't want to hang up. It could be the last time I would ever hear his voice or hear him declare his love.

I closed my eyes, willing my brain turn off, even for a few hours, but sleep eluded me. Visions of Ryker and me skated through my mind. Fragments of conversations rang in my ears. The feel of his fingers ghosting over my skin assaulted my senses. After minutes that moved like hours, I fell asleep.

Chapter Six

Ryker

Groaning, I clutched the sides of my skull. Why did I think it was a good idea to drink last night? I opened, then immediately closed my eyes. *What the hell?* The morning sun streamed through the open window. The next time I had a date with a bottle of tequila I needed to remember to shut the fucking blinds.

Bang.

And put in some earplugs. I curled my pillow around my head to block out the sound and the sun.

Bang.

"Ryker, are you awake?" Ignacio shouted through the door.

I added taping a *do not disturb* sign on the door to my list of things to do next time I drank too much.

"I'll be up in ten minutes. Leave me alone."

The door flung opening, clattering against the wall. "You should've been up two hours ago," Ignacio barked.

"Yeah. Yeah," I grumbled. I swung my legs over

the side of the bed. "What time is it anyway?"

"Almost nine o'clock in the morning."

I whipped my head around. "Seriously?" Over ninety-six hours had passed. My stomach rebelled, both from the tequila and the thought of Juan Alvarez torturing Hattie while I drank myself into a forced slumber. God, I was a fucking prick.

He nodded without saying a word.

I scratched the side of my neck. "Why'd you let me sleep so long?"

"I didn't realize you were still sleeping until twenty minutes ago."

I braced my head in my hands. It throbbed like a motherfucker. I drank one too many shots of bad tequila last night. I wasn't my finest moment, but I needed to do something to stop the regrets and guilt from circling in my brain like a bird of prey, waiting to devour me in a moment of weakness.

"How much time until the Americans get here?" I asked as I pulled yesterday's black shirt over my head.

"They're already here."

"A half hour early," I mumbled more to myself than him.

"Yeah, that's what happens when you offer double the normal rate. They don't want to piss you off."

I yanked my jeans up my legs and fastened the button. "I'm ready. Let's go."

Ignacio's dark eyes traveled the length of my body, and then he shook his head. "You look like hell."

"I feel like hell," I said as shoved my feet into

my shoes. "But it's nothing a cup of coffee won't fix."

"And you think it's still a good idea to charge into an Alvarez stronghold tomorrow?"

"Tonight."

"Emanuel said everything was going down tomorrow."

"Yeah, well, I changed my mind."

His nostrils flared as he sucked his lips into his mouth. "I don't like it."

"I don't have a choice."

He leaned against the doorjamb. "There's always a choice."

"No." I shook my head. "There's really not. I'm not going to leave Hattie there for a second longer than I have to." Also, I didn't fully trust Emanuel, so I'd misled him about my intentions for as long as possible.

Ignacio's lips twisted like he'd sucked on a lemon. "Then try to stop yourself from drowning in a bottle of tequila again today. I don't need a dead son. I need a son to help me with business. You need to hold up your side of the bargain. Acting like goddamn pussy won't help Hattie or me."

"Yeah, fuck you," I mumbled as I brushed by him. I couldn't argue with him. Not even a week after making this bargain with Ignacio and I was morphing into Rever—drinking too much, playing the victim card, and missing Hattie so much it felt like someone had taken a pickaxe and hollowed out my chest.

I missed her scent, her taste, her everything. I ached to touch her. Hold her. Kiss her. I used to believe she was my salvation. My home. My heart belonged to her. I'd tried to change my life and become a better person for her, but fate won. She couldn't be my anything. I was a danger to her life and the life of my unborn child.

I wanted to bury my fist in the wall, but with my luck I'd break my hand, and then I wouldn't be any help to Hattie. No, I needed to pull my head out of my ass. I didn't have the luxury of taking my aggravation out on the wall or Ignacio. I needed to stay focused and ignore the bitter pang of regret bubbling like a noxious poison in my midsection. I wasn't allowed to have feelings any longer. I couldn't afford to have feelings. I was indebted to the Vargas Cartel for the rest of my miserable life. Soon enough, I'd turn into a soulless, drug running murderer. I might as well get used to the twisted emptiness now.

"Are the Americans in your office?" I asked, clenching my fists.

"Yes."

My shoes clipped across the tiled floor. "Are you joining us?"

"Not today."

I whirled around. "Why not?"

"Let's just say, I'm not feeling up to it."

I scanned his body. He still looked weak. His skin was pale and dark smudges circled his eyes. He'd left the hospital last night, but only because he refused to stay in there another day.

"Okay. Do you need anything?"

"No, just rest."

I nodded, then crossed the living room and

opened the door to the study. Three men sat in the study across from Emanuel. Two had closely shaved heads and nearly identical white t-shirts and jeans. The man on the right, dressed entirely in black with longish hair, looked familiar, but I couldn't place him.

"Emanuel," I said as I slid into the only remaining chair.

"Ryker, I've already given them a brief summary of the mission." Emanuel replied. He poured coffee from a metal carafe into a clear glass mug. "Do you take your coffee black?"

"Sure. Thanks." I took a sip of the lukewarm coffee and then placed the mug on a carved wood side table. "Are you going to introduce us?" I asked, tipping my head in the direction of the three men on the leather sofa.

"You're right." Emanuel leaned forward in Ignacio's chair, bracing his elbows on the desk. "Where are my manners?"

I refrained from rolling my eyes. All five men sitting in that study, including me, didn't give a rat's ass about manners. I wanted to free Hattie. Emanuel wanted to please Ignacio, and the three men on the sofa wanted a shitload of untraceable money.

Unwilling to listen to Emanuel blow smoke up my ass all day, I stood up, intending to take control of the meeting. "I'm Ryker Vargas. I know Emanuel already knows your history, but go ahead and give me a short summary of your background before I share the details of this particular job."

"Noah Fiennes," the man on the right said.

"Former US Marine. I spent the last three years in the Middle East doing freelance work. I've been in Mexico for four months."

"Why did you relocate?" Making contacts as a freelance assassin was the hard part of the job. Most people stayed in the same area unless their cover was blown.

"I'm here doing some research that relates to my work in the Middle East. I figured I'd pick up some jobs while I'm here. I'm going back at the end of the year. Maybe sooner. I haven't decided."

My eyes narrowed. I knew what he was talking about. There'd been a lot of speculation lately about connections between drug cartels and Muslim extremists. As far as I knew, Ignacio hadn't allied with one, but at the end of the day, cartels were interested in making money, and with the seizure of oilfields in Iraq, Muslim extremists had a lot of it these days. "You look familiar."

"Yeah," he said with a practiced smile. "We met in passing, but you were Ryker Fallon, and I had a different name at that time too—Nazar Fayed."

I pursed my lips. "Right." I'd run into Nazar Fayed about three years ago. He was working undercover in some Muslim organization with alleged ties to terrorist groups. Unfortunately, he had ties to the US government. Something I didn't want for this mission. "So you're still working for the US government?"

He scoffed. "They've hired me a few times, but they'd never claim me. Consider me an equal opportunity consultant without moral hang-ups. I follow the money wherever it leads me. Sometimes that's the US government. Sometimes it's a drug cartel in Mexico. Other times, it's a Russian arms dealer or a fundamentalist organization."

"So you're a liability. If the Alvarez Cartel gave you more money, you'd flip sides mid-mission?"

"No," he spat. "I never quit mid-job. Once I'm in, I'm all in."

"Ah," I mocked, raising one eyebrow. "So you do have some morals."

"No, just a healthy sense of self-preservation. If I develop a reputation for flipping sides, I'd never get another job and I'd have an exponentially shortened life span."

My eyes narrowed into slits.

"He's telling the truth," Emanuel interjected, folding his arms across his chest. "We've hired all three of these men before. We've never had any problems, and their references check out. Ignacio investigated each one of them himself. I have the files if you want to review them at length."

I nodded. I believed him. Ignacio never did anything without meticulous planning and due diligence. Noah's situation was similar to mine when I worked as a fixer. I'd taken whatever job paid the most. Sometimes, I had worked indirectly for the US government or other governments, but I was never entrenched with one entity or person. While the steady work one government could provide was nice, it made a consultant beholden and dependent. Two things I never wanted to be.

I cringed inwardly. Somehow I'd ended up indebted and tied to the Vargas Cartel for the rest of my life. Just that fleeting reminder made me want to dive into another bottle of tequila. If Hattie were safe, I'd do exactly that. Alcohol had the benefit of blurring unpleasant truths.

I gestured to the other two men. "What about you two?"

"I'm Rick," the blond haired man seated in the middle said. "I did two tours in Afghanistan. I've been freelancing in Mexico for the last three years."

"Me too," the last man said. "Rick and I were in the military together. We've worked together a few times, but most of the time, we do our own thing. I'm Eric, by the way."

I walked the length of the room with my arms folded across my chest. These three men weren't the only ex-military, muscle-for-hire, in Mexico with adequate qualifications. With US unemployment at a high, particularly for military veterans, tons of ex-military personnel floated in and out of Mexico looking to make a quick buck. I could spend weeks interviewing potential candidates, but I didn't have weeks. Hattie could be dead in a matter of days. As a rule, I didn't trust anyone else's judgment, but right now I had to trust Emanuel and Ignacio.

I swiped a stack of papers from the desk and handed each one of the men a stack of photos of the Alvarez safe house. "Okay. This is where they're holding the hostage."

"When are we going to move on the location?" Noah asked as he studied the photos.

"Tonight," I answered.

"Don't you think we should do a little recon first?" Rick said, cocking his head to the side.

"That would be ideal, but time is of the essence."

Rick whistled as he shook his head.

I shot him a leveling stare. "Is that going to be a problem for you? If so, you can get the fuck out now. Either you're all in or you're not."

Rick scrubbed the side of his face. "You're asking us to take a leap of faith here. A lot can go wrong."

"You're absolutely right. This mission could blow up in our faces whether or not we spend a week staking out the Alvarez safe house." I paused in front of him, resting my hands on my hips. "Either way, I've agreed to compensate you for the added risk and time constraints. If it's not adequate, then you can walk out right now." I waved my hand toward the door.

Rick's lips curled. "This is a suicide mission. We don't know if the place is booby-trapped or how many men we'll encounter. At least let a few of us do a quick surveillance run tonight so we're not running blind."

"He has a point," Noah said, propping his ankle on the opposite leg. "The security might change the following night, but it'd give us more information than a few pictures."

"No," I spat, my hands shaking with violence. "If someone sees us, they'll move her or kill her and we'll be right back to square one, except they'll know we want her."

Noah's nostrils flared. "And if we fail because we're unprepared, they'll cut off her head and deliver it to her family or you by sunrise."

"Failing isn't an option." I curled my hands into

balls. "Are you saying you're not good enough to do this?"

Noah's lips thinned, and his eyes glittered. "No, I'll do it, but I want seventy-five percent of the money dropped into my account before I'll lift a finger."

I glanced out the window. An older man with gray hair crouched in the garden beds planting flowers. "Are you worried you're not going to make it out?"

"No. I always come out on top." He chuckled as he leaned back. "I'm worried you won't make it out and I won't be paid."

"I'm not worried about myself, but I'll wire the money to your account tonight."

"One more thing," Noah said.

"What's that?"

"The final twenty-five percent payment won't be dependent on whether the girl lives or dies."

"No." I gritted my teeth. "I need there to be an incentive for you to do everything in your power keep her alive."

Noah ran his fingers over his lips. "Fine, but if they kill her before we show up, I still want all the money you promised me."

A shiver ghosted down my spine. I hoped his words weren't prophetic. Hattie couldn't die. I wouldn't allow it. Life couldn't be that cruel. I swiped my hand across my forehead, hardening my heart. "Deal," I barked with a wintry smile. "Now, let's bang out the logistics so we can get everything ready."

Chapter Seven

Hattie

"Wake up."

A boot rammed into my lower back, not hard enough to injure me, but with enough force to get my attention. I scrambled to my knees and pushed my greasy, matted hair from my face. My stare collided with Enrique's, and I quickly lowered my gaze.

"Okay. Okay. I'm up," I mumbled.

"We're moving you to a new location today."

I chewed on my lower lip, stifling the questions stampeding like a herd of cattle through my mind. Instead, I nodded with half-lowered eyelids. Ryker promised he'd come for me tonight. Hopefully, Enrique intended to move me into another room inside this house rather than to a new location. Even if he moved me across the country, I wouldn't object too much. Twenty-four hours in a damp room with a decaying corpse was enough.

The toe of his black boot moved up and down as

he glared at me.

Tap, tap, pause.

Tap, tap, pause, and repeat.

"Get up. I have to remove your shackles."

As I stood up, I peeked at him from beneath the shield of my lashes. Looking at Enrique reminded me of staring at the devil. His teeth winked in the dim light, and an aura of menacing evil emanated from him. His dark eyes gleamed with an unholy light as he rubbed his palms together in anticipation of inflicting pain. Icy terror shot down my spine, and the air felt heavy against my chest.

"The new room doesn't have any restraints, but if you're a good girl, I won't handcuff you." He sucked his lips into his mouth. "If not, I'll have to improvise."

He started with the thick bands of metal around my wrists. He unlocked one and then the other. I closed my eyes, shivering in frozen silence as his sweaty hands coasted along my skin. Seconds later, he crouched at my feet, freeing both my ankles, and a heavy gasp fell from my lips.

I stepped to the side, but his hand closed around my ankle. I glanced at him as his fingers ghosted up the inside of my calf. The glide of his course fingertips branded my skin. Bile clawed up my throat. My muscles stiffened, and I coiled my hands into tight balls of fury. I couldn't breathe. When he reached the inside of my knee, I bit the inside of my cheek until the metallic taste of blood swirled around my mouth.

Oh my God. Oh my God. Please don't do this. Please don't let this happen. Please don't let him find the phone.

I should've fought.

I should've kicked.

I should've bolted for the door.

I should've screamed, but I didn't want to die.

A gun glinted from the waistband of his pants, turning every cell in my body to ice. I clamped my eyes shut as my mind whirled, searching for a happy memory, something to anchor me to my life away from this moment. Away from this evil.

Tremors hijacked my legs, slowly slithering up my body until my muscles rippled in nonstop waves of violence and disgust. My feet were rooted to the floor.

When his fingers reached the bottom of my running shorts, I couldn't take it any longer. Rage tore through me like a bolt of lightning, and I jerked my leg to the side. "Don't touch me," I spat through my teeth.

He cocked an eyebrow. "I thought we could have a little fun."

"Fuck you," I snarled.

A sinister smile slid across his too smug face. "That's exactly what I had in mind."

My gaze zipped around the room. Adrenaline pumped through my veins. My heart thundered erratically as if someone had pressed a defibrillator to my chest. Then, everything clicked into place, and I lunged for the door. I didn't know where it'd lead me. I didn't even know if I'd get more than ten steps before Enrique put a bullet through my back, but common sense fled in favor of dignity and self-respect.

When I reached the threshold, he fisted his hand in the tangled strands of my hair and wrenched me backward. Pins and needles exploded in my scalp.

"Where do you think you're going?" He punctuated each word with a tug of my hair, inexorably dragging me backward.

Hot tears prickled the corners of my eyes. My chest heaved like I couldn't catch my breath. Disjointed pants puffed from my mouth, bouncing off the concrete walls. Thousands of curses tumbled through my brain, but I didn't respond. I couldn't. I felt like I was drowning. What I wanted to do wasn't relevant.

"Get on your knees, *puta*." He slammed his hand between my shoulder blades and I tumbled face first onto all fours. Fire zigzagged up my limbs. My hair shrouded the sides of my face. Whimpers and incoherent pleas vomited from my mouth.

He whipped the gun out of his waistband. It dangled restlessly from his fingertips. His obsidian eyes seared my skin as he unbuckled his belt with one hand. The metal of the buckle rattled unnaturally through my ears. Next came the slide of leather that resembled the hiss of a snake. With a flick of his wrist, he opened his fly, and he shoved his pants down to his mid-thigh, exposing his red boxers.

"No. No. No," I murmured between broken sobs and trembling lips.

"Crawl over here. You need to earn your keep."

I shook my head violently from side to side. "No."

He lifted the gun and pointed it at my face. "Do

it or I'll pull the fucking trigger."

I glanced over my shoulder toward the open door. Then, my gaze slid down his body, my face carefully blank. "Go ahead. Kill me," I taunted as I came to my knees. I refused to do what he wanted. I wouldn't beg for mercy.

Enrique whipped his head from side to side, popping his neck. Then, a smile crept across his face.

"If you're holding out for Ryker Vargas, don't bother. He's not coming for you. He abandoned you, so you may as well enjoy your time with me."

My stomach rolled and I wrapped my arms around my waist, trying to hold together the fractured pieces of my courage. "You're wrong."

He tipped up his head and chuckled. "Ah, how cute. You really think he cares about you. You really think he loves you. He hasn't done a damn thing for over four days. If the Vargases had my woman, I wouldn't let a single day pass."

A tight smile curved my lips upward. "I don't think he loves me. I know he does. He'll come for me."

"Really?" His eyebrows vaulted up his forehead, and one side of his mouth hitched upward like he knew a dirty secret. "Then why did he tell us to do whatever the hell we wanted with you?"

I gasped.

He snickered. "He told us to go ahead and call your dad because he didn't give a shit what happened to you. He doesn't want anything to do with you. You're—and this is a direct quote—not worth the energy or the resources."

My stomach plunged. The edges of my vision blurred and spun in kaleidoscope-worthy circles. "You're lying," I hissed, feeling like my heart had flat-lined.

His hands circled my upper arms, and he tugged me flush against his body, my head slamming into his thighs. "Be a good little girl, and pull out my cock. You need to do something mind-blowing to convince me I should let you live a couple more days."

"Never." I gagged as my stomach convulsed, but nothing came out.

His hands gripped the collar of my shirt and tore it down the front. "I'm waiting," he said, trailing the pad of his thumb around the edges of my sports bra.

"You can keep waiting," I taunted, feeling reckless. Feeling like I didn't have any reason to live. If Ryker gave up on our baby and me, I didn't want to live.

At that moment, I didn't think I had much left to lose. Ryker told me he'd find me, but I might be dead by then. Fear could go fuck itself. I would have to be dead and cold, my soul long gone from this world before I'd willingly allow Enrique to use me.

Enquire pulled down his boxers and shoved his gun against the side of my head. "Do it."

"No," I screamed through my teeth.

Our eyes battled silently for a few exaggerated seconds. Then, heavy footsteps echoed down the hallway, but I refused to tear my attention from his face. I had to be ready for anything.

"What the hell are you doing?" Juan Alvarez

roared as he paused at the entrance to the room.

"What does it look like?" Enrique said, grinding his gun into the side of my head.

"I asked to you move her to a new location and meet me in the office. We don't have time for this shit today," Juan countered, his eyes slanted into razor like slits. "We have to get ready."

Relief tingled down my spine, and my body sagged.

"You heard him," Enrique barked as he kneed me in the chest. "Get up."

I tumbled onto my back and my head smacked against the concrete. Sweat sprung from my pores and pain vibrated inside my skull. Gasping, I rolled to the side and cupped the back of my head. Moisture spilled from the corners of my eyes. I wanted to disappear.

"Fuck," I grumbled.

My head hurt.

My muscles hurt.

My heart hurt.

Every inch of my body felt like I had been put through a meat grinder.

"Enrique," Juan growled, running his hands through his silver threaded hair. "I don't know what kind of game you're playing, but we have people waiting for us. If you want to play with her, come back tonight. I don't give a shit, but do it on your own time."

His words hit my chest like a pile of stones, and the air whooshed out of my lungs. My limbs trembled in waves with an excess of fear and adrenaline.

Juan tugged me to my feet by my arms. His fleshy fingers dug into my skin as I steadied myself.

"Walk!" Juan shouted as he cracked his knuckles like a prizefighter trying to intimidate his opponent. He shouldn't have bothered. I was already scared out of my mind. What happened at the Vargas Cartel compound was child's play compared to this.

"Okay. Okay," I mumbled as I stumbled to the door.

Enrique pulled up his pants without fastening the buckle. Then, he stomped by me pointing his gun at my face. "Follow me and don't do anything stupid."

We walked up a narrow set of concrete stairs. Light flooded the main floor of the house. I shaded my eyes with my hand as I sucked air into my lungs through my nose. I couldn't fill my lungs fast enough to clear the stench of death from my body. I'd been breathing through my mouth since Enrique shot Raul and left his body in the room with me.

"Are you sure you want her upstairs?" Enrique asked Juan, pausing at the base of the rust-colored tiled stairwell.

"Yes." Juan nodded. "Put her in the last room on the left and don't waste any more time."

Enrique spun around with his lips pursed. "I'm not an idiot. I heard you the first fucking time."

"If you heard me the first time, I wouldn't have walked into the room with your pants around your ankles and your cock hanging out."

"Gilipollas," Enrique murmured as he started walking up the stairs. His heavy boots thumped against the floor.

"Enrique, you're my oldest son. I love you, but

don't talk back to me or second-guess me again. Do what you're told and shut your fucking mouth."

Enrique's shoulders tensed, but he kept walking. I followed him. I didn't have a choice. The only thing keeping me from throwing myself down the stairs was Ryker's promise he'd find me tonight. A few more hours and this would be over. One way or another.

Enrique flung open the light brown wooden door. I halted, unsure what to do.

"What are you waiting for? A fucking invitation?" His rancid breath washed over my face.

"No." I shook my head as I stepped through the opening.

"Take a fucking shower. You smell like shit. I don't want to have to tie a bandana around my face when I come back for you tonight."

He slammed the door and locked it. The room was better than the basement. Almost anything would be better than being chained to a wall in a room with a dead body. I shivered.

The room had a twin-sized yellowed cot on a metal frame and a barred window on the far side of the room. I opened the door next to me. It was a small bathroom with floor to ceiling square sky blue ceramic tiles. A showerhead came out of the center of the ceiling with a rusted floor drain directly below it. A white wall-mounted sink and a toilet with a cracked seat were located on opposite walls.

Briefly, I considered refusing to shower so Enrique would leave me alone, but in the end I turned on the shower and stripped off my clothes.

My blood and Raul's blood mingled, staining my

hands and clothes. Sweat and dirt coated my skin. I couldn't comb through the snarled strands of my hair. I needed to scrub the memory of the last few days from my skin. Maybe then I could gain some much-needed clarity and perspective.

I stepped under the shower and cranked the rusted lever. The pipes banged against the wall. Icy russet colored water poured from the ceiling. My breath hitched and then evened out when the water warmed. I stood under the weak spray longer than I should have, given my circumstances, but a shower had never felt so good.

Chapter Eight

Ryker

"This is it. We're here," I said.

I pulled the black SUV over to the side of the road. As planned, the two SUVs behind us followed suit. I had divided us into three teams. Noah and I would hike up the side of the mountain and enter through the back door. Rick would wait here until I contacted him. He and his team would neutralize the men guarding the driveway. Eric and his team would hike up with Noah and me, and enter the safe house through the front door. Eric would engage and kill anyone in the building. Noah and I would find Hattie.

We had less than thirty minutes to accomplish everything once we broke down the doors. If we didn't make it out by then, we were fucked. Juan's reinforcements would show up, and the helicopters lifting us out of the remote location would flee or risk being shot down.

I picked up my gun from the center console and slid it into the holster around my chest. I slipped on the tactical headset. Then, I opened the car door and looped an X95 assault weapon around my shoulder. The X95 had quickly become my go-to gun. Israel Weapon Industries created the gun to combat modern terror threats.

"Ready?" I asked, tipping my head in the direction of the hill in front of us.

"Yep," Noah answered as he slipped a grenade into his black vest.

"Let's move." I motioned to Rick's SUV. He saluted. Then, I waved Eric and his team forward. "No talking on the headsets until we're inside."

Without further instructions, we disappeared into the foliage next to the street. We all knew our roles. We all knew what was at stake. No one could leave until we rescued Hattie.

Every step over the dense undergrowth sounded like a land mine detonating in my ears. My hands twitched. My heart thrashed inside my ribcage like a feral animal from a sickening concoction of fear and excitement.

In the past, I wasn't personally invested in the outcome of any mission. Sure, I wanted to be paid, and I wanted my client to be satisfied. After all, if things didn't work out, it'd look bad. But none of that compared to the emotions simmering like lava through my veins as I hiked up the hill. If I didn't walk out of the safe house with Hattie alive and well, I'd lose my shit. I'd kill every last member of the Alvarez Cartel, their family members, their friends and neighbors.

As I ate up the distance between Hattie and me, my insides festered with raw anger and my fingers itched for revenge. I forced every errant cell in my body to stay focused on the end goal. I conjured an image of Hattie in my mind.

Her soft smile.

Her topaz eyes.

Her long legs.

Her crisp, clean scent.

Her flawless skin.

She captivated my thoughts. She possessed my heart. She owned me. She'd always own me.

And I fucking ruined her. I abducted her. I manipulated her. I tainted her with my love, but not any longer. Once I rescued her and healed her, I'd set her free. I'd give her anything and everything she needed to have the perfect life she deserved. Then, I'd sever every last connection so she wouldn't have to worry about who'd come after her next.

My heart seized and then shriveled two sizes at the thought of living without her, but love meant sacrifice. I accepted it and tomorrow I'd embrace it. I pushed thoughts of the future out of my head and concentrated on the present.

I paused at the edge of the tree line, just out of the line of sight of the safe house. Dim yellow lights flickered from the windows, taunting me. I held up my open hand, signaling for everyone to stop. I crept forward, keeping inside the shadows, surveying the exterior of the building. After I had made a circle around the entire perimeter of the house, I lifted my hand, signaling that four people were outside the safe house. Then, I raised my arm above my head, pointing my index finger straight up and my thumb parallel to the ground, indicating the guards had rifles.

I didn't know what we'd encounter inside, but for now, we outnumbered them. I sucked in a gust of sticky, humid air, struggling to unravel all the twisted emotions and thoughts flitting through my mind. Conflicted emotions and dread of the future would only cloud my judgment. I needed to be unfeeling. Mechanical.

If Hattie were dead, I'd be irreversibly broken. Life wouldn't be worth living. If Hattie was alive, I had to destroy us, and I'd live the rest of my life without her. Either outcome would suck. At least if she were alive, I'd know I had done everything I could for her. She'd still be breathing the same air and inhabiting the same world as me. That had to count for something.

With a flick of my hand, I waved my piecemeal army forward.

Crouched low, I gripped my X95 and mentally flipped my middle finger at the angel of death. My soldiers flanked me in a u-shaped formation. I pointed toward the breaker box at the back of the house. Noah would flip the breaker, blanketing the safe house in darkness before we fired a single shot.

We moved stealthily forward, our black clothing and camouflage face paint blending into the inky night. Sweat prickled my skin. The hair on the back of my neck stiffened. My ears devoured the noise of every branch crunching under our booted feet, every exhalation whistling through the air, and every rustle of fabric against fabric as we forged ahead.

Time to get Hattie.

Time to destroy the Alvarez Cartel once and for all.

I'd kill every last one of them until I didn't have any strength left in my body.

With every step, anger sizzled in my veins. My lips curled up over my teeth as I inhaled through my nose. The thirst for revenge rippled through my muscles. I smashed every civilized thought from my brain. I courted the Vargas beast inside my soul until inhumane savagery pumped through my body.

The lights in the house disappeared, steeping us in total darkness.

It was show time.

Chapter Nine

Hattie

With my hair still damp, my eyes popped open. My heart fluttered. Springs dug into my back. I pushed onto my elbows. I didn't know what had woken me. I didn't know whether it was day or night. I recalled climbing into the cot wearing a threadbare, dingy robe when I finished showering, but after that, nothing.

I scrambled to my knees. My ears throbbed, desperately searching for the faintest noise. I scanned the room, diving in and out of the shadows looking for something. Anything. Anyone, but the room was as empty as I remembered.

Rubbing my eyes, I tipped my head to the ceiling. Then, I remembered Raul's phone. *Shit!* I forgot to turn it on.

I scrambled to my feet and darted across the room. My body buzzed with adrenaline as I unzipped the pocket of my shorts, pulled out the phone and powered it on. Air rocketed out of my lungs when I saw Ryker's text.

I'm coming for you tonight. Be ready.

Clutching the phone, I ran to the window and shoved the curtains to the side. I couldn't see anything. Crosshatched bars obscured the view and the miniscule rectangles of sky between looked like segmented inkblots. I ran back to the bathroom and slipped on my stained running shorts under my robe and waited.

At first, I thought something dropped on the floor. Then, the sound happened again. Rapid-fire gunshots exploded one after another outside.

Pop, pop, pop.

Pause.

Pop!

It was happening. Ryker was here. He came just like he promised.

Minutes crawled like hours, as I huddled next to the door waiting for Ryker to find me. I used the light from Raul's phone to illuminate the room. Gunshots blended into one long, deafening roar of violence. I twisted my hands in my robe over and over until the seam along the side split. My chest heaved in short bursts. I should've made an effort to regulate my breathing, but I was incapable of doing anything except staring at the door.

Then came the shouts, screams and cries of pain. Incoherent Spanish curses floated up the stairs. For the hundredth time in the last three or four months, I wished I had taken Spanish lessons instead of French.

"Pudrete en el infierno."

"Chingada Madre."

Fleetingly, I wondered what would happen if everyone died. Would I be stuck in this room until I died of starvation? Nobody except Ryker knew I was in Mexico. I told my parents I'd taken a road trip to clear my thoughts. Would the police or somebody else eventually show up? Or would the foliage grow over the building, entombing us in vines?

I surveyed the contents of the room, looking for a weapon. I flipped over the cot and kicked at the metal bars trying to free something. Nothing budged. I ran to the bathroom and switched on the light. Nothing happened. My hearted squeezed. Somebody had cut the power.

Squinting, I located the showerhead, then jumped and yanked on the metal arm protruding from the ceiling. Hanging on with all my body weight, I swung back and forth. The pipe creaked, and then I stumbled to my knees with the showerhead in my hand.

Pain radiated up my legs. Water exploded out of the pipe, spraying from the ceiling, drenching my clothes. Wet strands of hair slid in front of my eyes. Water leaked into my mouth.

"Fucking hell!" I screamed, shaking my head from side to side.

I crawled across the floor, back to the bedroom. I settled into the corner and curled into a ball. Water dripped from my robe. I squeezed the excess water from the ends. I could've slipped on my t-shirt, but wearing a transparent robe was infinitely more appealing than being covered in Raul's blood, my sweat, and days worth of dirt.

Then, I heard loud footsteps echoing down the hallway. The door handle rattled.

"Hattie," a voice I didn't recognize yelled.

I didn't answer. I scrambled to my feet and ran across the room. Standing next to the door, I raised the showerhead above my head preparing to strike whoever entered the room.

"Hattie," the man shouted again. "Are you in there?"

A few shouts echoed down the hallway punctuated by two gunshots.

"I'm with Ryker. He sent me to find you," the man persisted.

I shifted on my feet. "Prove it."

"Back away from the door. I'm going to shoot the lock."

"Where's Ryker?"

"He's taking care of some people downstairs. Move away from the fucking door. I don't have all day," he demanded.

"I'll wait for Ryker." I couldn't trust anyone except him. For all I knew, this guy could be a member of the Alvarez Cartel or some other cartel wanting to get in on the action.

"Goddamn. What the hell is wrong with you? We need to get the fuck out of here. I'm not standing outside this door waiting for someone to kill me."

"I don't trust you. I don't trust anyone except Ryker."

"You're going to get us killed. Vargas," the guy screamed as heavy footsteps burst down the hall. "She won't move away from the door."

"Hattie, it's me," Ryker said. "Move to the right side of the door."

"My right or your right?"

"Yours."

With my body pressed into the wall, I scrambled to the other side of the door. "I moved."

"Now listen to me…" Ryker kept talking, but I couldn't hear him over the sudden roar of a helicopter over the house. With my eyes trained on the door, I cupped my hands over my ears.

"Who's that? What's going on?"

He didn't answer.

Sparks ricocheted off the door. Then, it flew open, bouncing off the adjacent wall.

"Watch our back," Ryker shouted, pointing to the man in the shadows.

In the darkness, I could make out the outline of Ryker's body. I ran across the room and circled my arms around his strong shoulders. My fingernails dug into the back of his neck like talons. My knees sagged. Tears flooded my eyes. My breath came hard and fast until I started hyperventilating.

He wrapped an arm around my waist, and his fingers pressed into my side. "Relax, Hattie. I've got you."

He rocked me back and forth for a frozen second, and I wanted to tell him I missed him, I loved him, I couldn't live without him, and so much more. But the words wouldn't come. Instead, I pressed my lips to his neck, drawing his essence into my lungs. He smelled like sea air, gunpowder and man, but somehow it was better than anything in the world.

"Can you walk?" he whispered, next to my ear.

Jumbled thoughts whirled through my mind. Incoherent words mixed with whimpers streamed from my mouth. I couldn't think. I couldn't talk. Walking was out of the question.

"Listen, baby. We need to get out of here right now. The helicopter can only stay so long before it draws too much attention."

I lifted my head from his chest and nodded. "I can walk."

"Hold on to the back of my belt and don't let go no matter what happens."

I clamped my hands around his belt, fusing my body to his. My swollen hand protested the movement, but I ignored the pain. "Got it," I whispered, my throat raw from dehydration and crying for days.

"Noah," Ryker said. "Follow us out of here."

A tall, dark-haired man stepped out of the shadows. A flash of light from the bottom of the stairs lit up one side of his face. He had sharp cheekbones, a long angular nose and almond shaped eyes. He flashed a thumbs-up signal. "I'm on it."

With his gun in front of him, we jogged down the stairs. Dead bodies and bloodied groaning men littered the floor. I floated through the room as if I were submerged in water, suffering from a nightmare I couldn't wake up from. My vision tunneled. My entire body trembled so I hard I thought I'd collapse.

"Don't look. Just keep your gaze glued to the ground in front of you and keep putting one foot in front of the other," Ryker said without glancing at me.

I squeezed my eyes shut and plastered my body against his back. My fingers curled around the waistband of his pants. My lungs rattled with suppressed cries. I would've crawled inside him if it were possible. A warm breeze caressed my skin. We were outside. Relief poured through my body. I opened my eyes and lifted my head to the sky, drinking in the faint glimmer of the stars. Palm trees danced in the wind. Sea salt wafted through the air. On any other night, it would've been peaceful, but not today. With the roar of the helicopter blades slicing through the air, it felt sinister. Ominous.

Three guys barreled around the corner of the house, their guns pointed at us. *"Ya están aquí."*

Ryker shoved me away from him, and I stumbled backward. "Noah, get her the fuck out of here. Now!"

"No," I repeatedly screamed, reaching for Ryker. Horror clawed at my chest, dragging me into a full-blown panic attack within a matter of seconds. I didn't want to be separated from Ryker ever again.

Noah wrapped his arms around my waist and heaved me over his shoulder. "No. I'm not leaving him. Leave me here." I slapped the corded muscles of his back until my hands stung.

"You don't have a choice," Noah growled.

"Please," I begged, as my heart crumbled. "I can't leave him. Not again."

"It's better this way."

Noah ran to the helicopter, his boots kicking up a fine powdery dust that coated my lips. My head bounced against his back and blood rushed through my ears. Sobs clogged my throat. Acid gnawed at my gut. When we reached the door, he climbed inside and slammed it behind us. "We're ready to go."

"No. We can't leave him." I darted for the door, but Noah's arms closed around my waist and he pulled me into his lap.

Sickness twisted my insides. My heart beat like a pogo stick against the inside of my chest. I kicked, bit and slapped him, but he wouldn't budge.

"Shh," Noah whispered next to my ear. "Stop fighting. This is what Ryker wanted. You'd only be in his way."

"No." I lurched forward and elbowed him in the ribs.

He grunted, but his arms didn't relent. "For fuck's sake, you need to relax and let us do our job. We know what we're doing. Don't make this even more of a mess than it already is."

The energy drained from my body, and I slumped into his chest, my hands coiled into his black shirt. I didn't want to leave without Ryker, but Noah was right. There's nothing I could do to help him except do what he asked and get out of his way.

Chapter Ten

Ryker

With my gun pointed in the center of Enrique's Alvarez's chest, I pulled the trigger.

Click.

And…nothing.

I was out of ammunition.

Fucking hell.

Enrique tipped his head to the sky and howled like a coyote. "I've got this," he said to the men next to him. Go take care of my dad." He waved his high-powered rifle over my head. "The helicopter is leaving without you. Should I shoot it down?"

I eyed his rifle. It wouldn't come close. "That's not happening."

He shrugged. "Yeah, I guess you're right. I'll settle for killing you instead."

"You can try," I answered. I kept my voice steady even as nerves zigzagged through my body like a plasma ball.

"It's only fair. You tried to kill me last week. Now I'll return the favor, but unlike you, I'll actually succeed." He angled his chin to the side. "I already had some fun with your woman over the past few days, but I'm happy to show you some love too." He pointed his gun at my foot. "I think I'll start with your feet so you can't go anywhere. Then, I'll take my time. You know, make a real production of the whole thing. Maybe I'll burn a letter A into your arm so you match her."

Pain wailed through my chest. My blood ran cold. I glowered. "What the fuck did you say?"

"I guess you didn't look at her too closely." He shook his head, his dark eyebrows raised. "I branded your whore. You won't live long enough to appreciate it, but you'll die knowing I've marked her as property of the Alvarez Cartel. You may have rescued her, but she'll remember me for the rest of her life. This question is…will she remember you in a couple of years?"

My heart detonated like a grenade inside my chest. I didn't think. I couldn't think. Everything turned red. Rage fueled my body. I charged forward. My fist collided with his chin, and my knuckles scraped across his teeth.

Crack.

He stumbled backward, cupping the side of his face. I didn't give him the chance to retaliate. I circled my arms around his body and tackled him. Air exploded out of my lungs as we hit the ground.

I crawled up his body, pounding his face over and over until ribbons of blood gushed from his mouth and nose. With every hit, I relished his grunts of pain and the way his eyes went from alert to glazed.

Then, he slipped a knife from his pocket. I almost missed the glint of metal as he slashed his arm in a wild arch, connecting with my lower ribs. I grabbed his wrist, shoving the blade away from me. The bloody knife was suspended between our bodies as we fought for control. With my jaw clenched, our arms locked together, moving back and forth in a tug of war punctuated by grunts, groans, and unintelligible curses.

"I'm going to kill you," he snarled between grunts, his contorted face gleaming with sweat. His lips curled over his bloodied teeth like a wild animal. "Then I'm going after your woman."

With his free hand, he swiped the side of my cheek, raking his fingernails down my face to my neck. I winced and softened my grip on him. He seized the moment. He lurched forward trying to sit up, bringing his face within striking distance of mine. Without a second thought, I whipped my head forward, slamming my forehead into the bridge of his nose with a sickening crack. Blood spurted out of his nose, spraying my face.

Enrique's body went slack, and his head bounced like a basketball against the ground. His eyes rolled up in his head. I picked the knife off the grass, intending to carve a V in his cheek. I didn't know if I'd let him live, but he branded Hattie so I'd brand him.

Just as I finished the first gash in his cheek, someone yanked on the collar of my vest.

"We have to get out of here now! The SUVs are waiting for us at the end of the driveway," Rick said. "We're running out of time. Eric intercepted a call for backup."

"One more minute," I answered without glancing over my shoulder. I needed to finish this. If Enrique lived, he'd wear the Vargas V for the rest of his life. If he died, his family wouldn't want to have an open casket funeral.

My heart hammered inside my chest as I jabbed the tip of the knife into his cheek and slashed downward until the two lines intersected, perfecting the V. I wiped the handle of the knife on my pants and tossed it in the bushes next to the house.

I stood and kicked Enrique in the ribs. "Let's get the fuck out of here."

I turned to Rick. Dumbfounded, he rubbed his hand across his mouth, his eyes wide.

"What crawled up your ass?" I snapped.

"Nothing." He shook his head.

I started walking. "Are you coming?" I said as I glanced over my shoulder.

"Yeah, man." He jogged to catch up with me, his gaze glued to the side of my face like he'd never seen me before.

"What?" I barked.

"With your background, I assumed you wouldn't be as crazy as the rest of those cartel fuckers."

"You shouldn't assume anything. I'm a Vargas." I shot him a bitter smile as I rounded the side of the SUV.

"Aren't you going to finish that shit?" Rick asked, leaning his shoulder into the SUV.

"Finish what?"

"You need to kill that fucker or he'll hunt you down and go after Hattie again."

I spun around, eyeing Enrique's huddled body. He had rolled to his side, curling into a ball with his hand pressed to his cheek. My need for revenge had fizzled marginally in the last few minutes, but then I remembered the look on Hattie's face before Noah threw her over his shoulder. The way her body trembled and her eyes dilated scared the shit out of me. Her high-pitched cries would haunt me for years.

"You're right." I grabbed Rick's gun from his hands, aimed and pulled the trigger.

Once.

Twice.

Three times.

I handed him the gun and flung open the driver's side door. "Move. I'm driving."

Eric eyed me guardedly, and then he nodded. "Whatever you want. This is your show," he mumbled as he climbed into the passenger seat.

Chapter Eleven

Hattie

I pushed up, bracing my body on my elbows as my eyes scanned the darkness swallowing the room. The floorboards squeaked. A loud scream erupted from my mouth, ringing in ears. Arms circled around my waist. I swung my hands and my open palms connected with flesh. I curled my fingers into weapons, clawing at everything within my reach.

Someone pinned my arms to my sides. Short panting breaths exploded from my mouth. Fear crawled up my throat, suffocating me. My muscles stiffened, preparing for battle.

"Shh. It's me. It's Ryker," he whispered next to my ear. "You're safe. You're going to be okay."

I inhaled his familiar spicy sea scent, and the tension in my muscles evaporated. My heart slowed and my sluggish brain cleared. "Where am I?"

He didn't say anything for a few drawn out seconds. Instead, he stroked the back of my head lazily as he hummed softly in my ear. "You're in my room at my dad's compound."

As much as I hated the Vargas compound and everything it symbolized in my mind, relief zipped through my veins. I was safe here. Nothing would happen to me. Ryker would make sure of it. I cradled my head against his chest, savoring the moment. Savoring our connection. He rocked me back and forth silently. His strong, even heartbeat echoed in my ears, grounding me in the moment and away from the nightmare of the past few days.

"You should go back to sleep. You need your rest." His fingertips slid down my sides, and the bed shifted as he stood.

"Where are you going?"

"I'll be in the room next door if you need me."

I gasped and held out my hands, reaching for him. "Wait. Don't leave me. I don't want to be alone."

He tucked my hair behind my ear. "You need your rest," he repeated.

"I won't be able to sleep if you're not here."

"You did just fine without me. I'll just get in your way."

My brows furrowed as my mind scrambled to unravel his words. What was I missing? Something wasn't right.

"No." I shoved the sheets off my body. "Now that you're here, I'm not letting you go again."

"Hattie." My name came out like a long drawn sigh.

"Ryker," I responded in kind, kicking my legs over the side of the bed.

"When did you become so stubborn?" he mumbled more to himself than me.

I flipped on the light next to the bed. I searched his eyes for the glow of the affection I'd grown to love, but there was absolutely nothing. A blank void. A mask.

"What's going on right now? Why are you running away from me? Did I do something wrong?"

"No. Of course not," he said, his voice strained. His gaze bounced everywhere except on me.

"Then why won't you look at me?" I grabbed his wrist. He glanced at the A Enrique burned into my arm, and then he looked away like he couldn't stand the sight of me. I snorted. "You can't be serious."

"What?" he growled, the muscle in his jaw ticking. "I didn't do anything."

"You're right. You didn't." I dropped his arm and stood up. "You don't have to. It's written all over your face." I shook my head. "I get it. Explanations aren't needed."

My legs wobbled from disuse and exhaustion as I walked to the bathroom. I lamented my fate, the last three months, meeting Ryker, dating Evan…everything. At that moment, I hated myself. I hated my life. Why did everyone use me and reject me?

"You don't understand anything."

"Uh huh. Whatever," I mumbled.

"Where are you going?"

"To the bathroom to shower." I peeked over my shoulder. He alternated between flexing and curling his hands into tight balls. Obviously, our relationship had run its course—at least in his mind. He made me all these promises, and now he couldn't even look me in the eyes. "Don't worry about me. I'll be fine. Go back to your room and do whatever you were doing."

"No. Wait. I'll stay. Let me help you."

"Not if you're going look at me like you're going to be sick." I didn't turn around. I kept walking. I didn't want to see the pity or disgust flashing across his face like a neon sign.

His arms circled my waist and he dragged me against his chest. "You have no idea what you're talking about."

My body battled with my mind. My body wanted to sink into his embrace and beg him to never let go. My mind wanted to fight him, scream at him, and curse him to hell.

"The look on your face says it all, but I don't get it. Even Noah was more compassionate than you, and I'll probably never see him again. You, on the other hand, can't run away from me fast enough. You made me all these promises. Promises you have no intention of keeping. Are you going to ship me back to Evan again? Is that what this is about?"

He spun me around so fast, I felt like I had vertigo. "All this is my fault. I should've let you go. I should've stayed far away from your engagement party. Look at what I've done to you."

"Are you talking about this?" I held up my arm, waving the still pink and puckered letter A above my head.

He swallowed and nodded.

"Well, I don't give a shit about it. Just like everything that happened over the last few days, it will fade. It can be fixed. Everything can be fixed. I only care about us and our future." I'd spent every moment of the last five days reliving our moments together and dreaming of being with him again and he was pushing me away...again.

"You're right," he murmured, guiding me into the bathroom by my shoulders. "We'll take this one day at a time."

He turned on the bath and poured some bath salts into the water. Without meeting my eyes, he pulled my t-shirt over my head and slipped my panties down my legs swiftly and without a comment. Goosebumps kissed my greedy skin, and I swayed on my feet. My soul wept for his touch. His kindness. His love.

The second the bath filled, he tipped his head toward the tub. "Get in and relax."

For an uneasy second, I stared at his face, willing him to see me...really see me. I wanted him to tell me he still loved me. I wanted him to promise me we'd have a family and grow old together. Words circled the tip of my tongue like marbles, but nothing came out. I didn't know where to start.

He sighed heavily and combed his hands through his inky hair. My gaze fixated on the slight tremor. It was the only indication he still cared. Any sane girl would have run away a long time ago. But here I was, exposing myself to more heartache, praying he wouldn't push me away again.

"Just leave it alone for tonight," he whispered. "We'll talk tomorrow. Just get in and let me take care of you. I need to take care of you."

My shoulder muscles crawled up my neck. I wanted to talk to him. I needed to talk to him. Every passing second another emotional door slid shut between us. By tomorrow, I'd need a battering ram to get through to him. "Tell me what you're thinking."

"Please," he whispered, briefly shuttering his eyes. "Don't fight me on this."

A weighty exhalation whistled through my lips, releasing hundreds of unsaid words. He was right. I was tired. I ached. My arm still throbbed.

Wordlessly, I slipped into the bathtub. A moan tumbled from my lips without my permission, and my eyes fluttered closed like butterfly wings. Steaming hot water lapped around my neck. God, this felt amazing. I could sit here for hours.

"Are you hungry?" he asked.

I rolled my head from side to side without opening my eyes. "No. Noah brought me a plate of food before I fell asleep."

His feet shuffled on the tiles. "Good. A doctor will be here tomorrow to take a look at your injuries." He cleared his throat. "And to do an ultrasound."

My eyes cracked open, and I raised my injured arm out of the water. "My arm and hand are hurt, but other than that, I think I'll be okay. The ultrasound can wait until we get home."

"It's already scheduled and I'm concerned about you. Both of you."

"Okay." I shrugged. "When are we flying home?"

For strangled beats, he stared blankly at the wall, the expression on his face tough to interpret.

"Ignacio's jet will take you home the day after

tomorrow."

"I can't wait to leave." My eyes slid closed again. "Are you glad we're done with this place?"

He kissed my forehead. "Dunk your head under the water," he said, not answering my question. "Let me wash your hair."

The bumps of my spine tapped against the acrylic tub as I plunged into the warm water. When I surfaced, Ryker squirted shampoo into his hand and massaged it into my scalp. Thirty seconds later, all my confusion melted away. I didn't want to worry about tomorrow or next month. I wanted to enjoy this moment with him.

Cupping his hands together, he dribbled water over my head again and again until my hair was free of suds.

"Thanks," I said.

"My pleasure. It's the least I owe you."

"You don't owe me anything."

"I do. This was my fault."

Tears leaked from the corners of my eyes, silently trailing down my face. "I forgive you."

He stared icily at the floor, looking stricken. "I wouldn't blame you if you hated me."

I traced the line of his jaw, and he inhaled sharply. The sides of his face hollowed, and his chiseled cheekbones stood out in sharp relief. His thick eyelashes sheltered his gray eyes. The symmetrical arch of his top lip begged to be kissed.

"Get in here with me," I pleaded, unwilling to accept his need for distance any longer.

The corners of his lips curled upward, but he didn't say anything. He dipped his bruised and battered hands into the water and curled them around the curved lip of the tub. "I don't want to rush anything. We have time."

Craving him, I chewed on my lower lip, and then I tugged on the collar of his shirt. "No. I need to be close to you right now."

I needed to feel connected to him.

I needed to know the Alvarez Cartel hadn't destroyed us.

I needed to feel his hands on me and wipe Enrique's touch from my mind.

I wanted to be wanted.

I wanted to be normal.

Is that so bad?

Staring at me almost reverently with heavy eyelids, he rubbed his hands together. I wanted him so much that I stopped breathing for a suspended second. I was in agony. He groaned softly, gripping the edge of the tub. "Hattie, I don't think—"

I shifted onto my knees and looped my arms around his neck. Rivulets of water streamed down my body. Goosebumps somersaulted down my arms. A mixture of desire and something indecipherable glowed in his eyes. Hypnotic lust wove through my veins.

"Don't think, Ryker. Just kiss me. Make me forget. I need to forget, and you're the only one who can help me do that."

Chapter Twelve

Ryker

Everything moved in slow motion as Hattie's body rose out of the water like Botticelli's Birth of Venus. Like so many times since I first saw her, I struggled not to reach out and touch her.

The muted light of the bathroom highlighted her golden eyes. They glimmered like twin gemstones. Water dripped from the tips of her pink nipples. For a spine-tingling second, her unassuming seductive beauty immobilized me. She looked fragile with the faint bruise staining her cheek, but at the same time, I couldn't remember a moment when I wanted her more. I never wanted to forget the love and trust vibrating from her when I finally destroyed us.

I shuddered the instant she wrapped her arms around me. The recriminations in my head quieted to a dull hum. I sucked in a breath, scrambling to find the will to stop this. All the reasons I needed to let her go floated through my mind, but like tendrils of smoke I couldn't latch onto any of them. It all came down to one thing: I was bad for her. If I kept her in my life, the days she'd spent as a prisoner of the Alvarez Cartel would pale in comparison to a lifetime in the web of the Vargas Cartel.

I'd trade my soul to the devil to go back in time and change the way things unfolded, but it wasn't possible. I had to make the best decision for Hattie based on the facts, and the best decision was to send her away. I needed to force her out of my life even if the thought alone cleaved my heart in two. I didn't see any other way.

My fingers ghosted over the burn marks on her arm and her eyelids fluttered. "I don't want to hurt you." Her lips feathered across mine and electricity shot down my spine. I bit back a groan. Dammit, she was hard to refuse—more so now than the first time I met her. My need for her grew every day.

She rested her forehead against mine. "The only way you could hurt me is by leaving me," she said, her eyes glistening.

My throat tightened at the soft tenor in her voice. My soul devoured her words even though she was wrong. Leaving her was the only way to stop the pain and prevent future heartache, but when she looked at me with love shining from her eyes, reality and desire blurred.

"Hattie," I whispered, my voice like gravel on glass. It sounded like a benediction mixed with a curse. Half dark. Half light. It captured my character, my life, and my future perfectly.

She flicked open the buttons of my shirt, one after another, and pushed it off my shoulders. She licked her lower lip and my entire body trembled. I wanted her, but my desire for her didn't stop the guilt from wrapping around my chest like a vice. I shouldn't do this. I shouldn't touch her, but with every brush of her fingertips, my resistance evaporated faster than rain on hot asphalt.

Her fingertips coasted over the rectangular bandage on my ribs. It concealed the knife wound inflicted by Enrique Alvarez.

"What happened?"

"A small cut," I hissed as her hand pressed against the bandage. "Nothing you need to worry about. I'll be fine."

"Good. I don't want to be gentle." She opened the button of my pants, and I forgot everything but the sound of her breath next to my ear and the soft slide of her lips against my neck. In the blink of an eye, I had convinced myself we could share this last moment before real life bashed us over the head and demolished everything we'd worked so hard to build over the last few months. It was selfish of me, but I didn't want to fight this any more than I wanted let her go. There'd be plenty of time to sort this out tomorrow.

Groaning, I shoved my pants and boxer briefs down my legs and climbed into the tub with her. I pulled her into my lap and wrapped her legs around my waist. She smelled like soap, shampoo, sunshine, and everything Hattie. I ached to fill her again and make her believe in me, in us, no matter how fleeting the emotion.

"God, Hattie. You have no idea how much I missed you," I said, resting my forehead against hers.

Hot steam swirled around our bodies, cocooning

us in a world where only the two of us existed. I cupped her breasts, and she arched into me. Heat surged through my nerve endings making every point of contact between our bodies flame to life.

"Show me," she moaned.

Leaning back, my cock slid along her slippery sex. My last shred of common sense fled, and my mouth crashed against hers. Her tongue captured mine within seconds, and we devoured each other. My head spun from her familiar taste. Stopping was no longer an option. My muscles pulled tight like the string of a bow and sweat beaded on my forehead from the heat of the water. Urgency coursed through my veins like my soul knew this might be the last time I'd ever hold her.

The last time she looked at me as her savior.

The last time she surrendered to me unconditionally.

The last time she loved me.

If I concentrated hard enough, I could almost hear the minute hand of our life together counting down to the end of us. Maybe time had conspired against us from the first moment her beautiful golden eyes landed on mine.

Reverently, my hands cupped her breasts and then skated along her ribcage to her waist. Her back arched in invitation, and I had to taste more of her. I sucked her nipple in between my teeth. A gasp exploded out of her mouth, and I grazed her sensitive skin with my teeth.

"Ryker," she moaned, and I switched my attention to her other breast.

Licking.

Sucking.

Biting.

Showing her that this moment was about pleasure and pain, rather than just pleasure because, for me, that was exactly how it felt.

Pleasure that I could touch her one final time.

Pain that I had to let her go.

Within minutes, her entire body tensed like a coiled spring, vibrating with need as she rode the edge right along with me. Erotic whimpers tumbled from her mouth one after another until they blended into a symphony punctuating every lick, bite, suck and swivel of my hips. Desire and need hummed through my veins like morphine.

I couldn't wait another minute.

I had to be inside of her.

I had to feel the perfection of us.

I captured her mouth with a mind-drugging kiss. Every flick and roll of my tongue told her without words that I belonged to her even if I couldn't be with her.

Her hand snaked between our bodies and circled my length, sliding up and down in slow, lazy strokes. A desperate moan spilled from my mouth. Fuck that felt good. I closed my eyes and rocked my hips, but it wasn't enough.

The pads of my fingers trailed down her waist, following the line of her body to her sex. Simultaneous groans tumbled from our mouths as I slid my finger inside of her. I moved in and out of her slick entrance.

"Do you like that?" I asked even though I knew she did. She was flushed and trembling. Her chest heaved with every breath.

"God yes," she mumbled as her water-kissed lashes fluttered closed.

Her moans grew louder and louder with every pass of my fingers. Her facial expressions reprioritized my thoughts until I was hyper focused on her and her only.

Her parted lips.

Her heavy eyelids.

Her glowing skin.

She couldn't have looked more beautiful if she tried.

Just as her muscles contracted around my fingers, I pulled my hand away.

"No," she whispered, her pupils dilated.

"Shh. Don't worry. I've got you." I lifted her hips and pressed the head of my cock against her sex, sliding it back and forth. "I want to be inside you when you come."

"Mm." She nodded as she bit down on her lower lip. Her gaze dropped as I lowered her hips, her lips kicking up into a hedonistic smile.

"See," I said as lowered her slowly, watching until I disappeared inside of her. I felt like I was home again. No matter what happened she'd always belong to me and I'd belong to her.

A shaky exhalation whizzed through her lips, and I held my breath trying to control the need to claim her like a man possessed. I counted the seconds, giving her time to get used to me.

One.

Two.

Three.

And then, her walls clenched around my shaft, and my entire body shuddered. I didn't even need to move to be on the verge of exploding. *Fuck it.* I bucked my hips up and down in time with her, and her breasts bounced. I clenched my jaw, trying to stave off the lust roaring like a ball of fire through my body.

My hands bit into her hips, and we rolled together. Water splashed over the rim of the tub. Her golden skin flushed pink. Her nipples hardened into tight raspberry buds that made my mouth water. Our jagged breaths echoed off the marble tiles.

Her body undulated as my fingers dug into her hips. I gave her everything I had. Going slow wasn't an option. I forced us higher and higher until it felt like we were flying in a blur of bliss. Pleasure built at the base of my spine and static buzzed in my ears. I desperately needed to come, but I wouldn't go without her. If this was our last time together, I wanted her to remember it.

I reached between her legs, rubbing energetic circles on her clit. Her movements became frenzied. Then, her muscles tensed, and a scream tore from her lips. I couldn't stop my orgasm if someone had a gun pressed to my head. My muscles knotted, and I tipped over the edge with her. Satisfaction mixed with the emotional pain of goodbye ripped down my spine. My groans wrapped around her pleasure-laced cries.

When our orgasms faded, I lifted her out of the tub and carried her back to my bed.

I tucked her damp hair behind her ears. "Now you can sleep."

Smiling lazily, her hand clamped around my waist. "Stay until I fall asleep. I don't want to be alone anymore. I need you."

My heart squeezed and despite my better judgment, I crawled in next to her. The minute my head hit the pillow, the last five days slammed into me like a wrecking ball. More than ever, I regretted the need to force Hattie out of my life, but I didn't have a choice. I had to break her heart. I just hoped I'd be able to make it up to her somehow.

I lay quietly, bone deep tiredness claiming my limbs. My body begged me to sleep. I closed my eyes and drew her into my arms, my hard thighs pressing into her back and one arm possessively positioned around her waist. I promised myself I'd do what needed to be done tomorrow. Right now, Hattie was safe, and she was still mine. That's all that mattered.

Chapter Thirteen

Hattie

The heavy coffee colored wood door to the bedroom opened. The hinges whined.

"Miss Covington, are you awake?" Ignacio asked, peeking inside.

I yanked the sheets up to my neck. "Yes."

I couldn't find my suitcase or anything belonging to me, so I put on one of Ryker's t-shirts about an hour ago. The lack of adequate clothing kept me from roaming the house. I kept thinking Ryker would come to check on me any minute, but he hadn't.

"Good," Ignacio said, opening the door fully and walking to the foot of the bed. "Ryker arranged for a doctor to come to my house and check on you." He pointed toward the opening. "This is Dr. Mendez. He's a good friend of the family. He'll take care of you."

I chewed on the inside of my cheek as an older man entered the room, holding a black leather bag in one hand and a gray rectangular case in the other.

"Nice to meet you." The doctor smiled, revealing intricate webs lining the corners of his eyes.

"Mucho gusto," he answered with a quick nod of his head.

Ignacio shifted on his feet. "I don't anticipate any language issues. Dr. Mendez speaks English, but I can stay if you'd like."

Heat flooded my face, and my stomach flipped. I didn't know if Ryker told him about the pregnancy, but I didn't want him to find out this way. "No. I think I'll be okay."

"All right." Ignacio's shoes clipped over the tiled floor as he walked toward the door.

"Wait." I sat up and rested my elbows on my knees. "Can you send Ryker in? He'd want to be here."

Rubbing his hand along his jaw, his eyes met mine, then flicked away just as quickly. "He's not here right now."

"Oh." My stomach plummeted, and my fingers curled into the creamy white sheets until they strangled the circulation to my fingers. One more twist and I'd rip a hole in them. "Can you call him? I'd feel more comfortable if he were here. I'd do it myself, but I don't have a phone. I lost it when everything happened. Is there a phone in…?" My voice trailed off, and I licked my lower lip.

I was rambling. Ignacio knew it. I knew it. The freaking doctor knew it, but I couldn't stop myself. I felt like one of those colorful betta fish alone in a glass bowl. Both of them stared at me like I was about to snap. Maybe I was.

"He told me to tell you he'd be unavailable for

the majority of the day. He said he'll catch up with you tonight sometime."

I blinked repeatedly as I struggled to fend off the tears burning in the corners of my eyes. "What's that supposed to mean?"

Ignacio sighed. "Miss Covington—"

"Hattie," I shouted. "You know my name. You don't have to pretend like we're strangers. I've been here before. Tell me what's going on!"

I didn't understand why I said it. Truly, I didn't care what Ignacio called me. I didn't care if I ever saw him again. I hated him. In a roundabout way, his greed and corruption resulted in me becoming a hostage twice—once by him and once by the Alvarez Cartel. As far as I was concerned, he could jump off a cliff. I wouldn't shed a single tear.

Ignacio rocked back and forth on his heels, and the doctor's gaze ping-ponged back and forth between the two of us. He didn't even try to hide his surprise. I guess most people didn't talk to Ignacio like that given his penchant for murdering people.

"Hattie." Ignacio cleared his throat. "This is a conversation you should have with Ryker. It's not my place."

"But you know something, right?"

"All I'm going to say is that he won't be back for a while. Beyond that, you'll have to talk to him directly. It's not my place."

I shivered, trying to ward off the sudden chill racing down my spine despite the balmy breeze from the open windows. I stared at the woven ceiling fan as it rotated in slow circles. A faint buzz hummed through the room.

I'd hoped Ryker would want to spend the day with me. I needed him, more now than ever. I was scared out of my mind about so many things, but now I feared he planned to abandon me. Ignacio had never held his tongue before. That he felt the need to do so now could only mean Ryker had given up on me. Our baby. Us. My vision tilted as the realization slammed into me like a swift punch to my gut.

My gaze drifted to Dr. Mendez. His greedy eyes darted around the room, drinking in my anguish like a glass of ice water on a hot day. I swallowed hard, making a heroic effort to stifle my rising dread.

"Right," I said, my voice flat. "Do you know if my suitcase is around here somewhere? I'd like to get dressed so I can go for a walk later."

"No. Not today," Ignacio answered.

My eyes narrowed, and my heart drummed to a panicked beat. "So, I'm a prisoner again. Is that what you're trying to say? Here, I thought Ryker rescued me, but I guess I just exchanged one sadist cartel warden for another one."

"Dr. Mendez, can you step outside for a minute?"

"Por supuesto."

"Those are Ryker's rules, not mine," Ignacio said after Dr. Mendez stepped into the hall. "You can take it up with him. If it were up to me, I'd have you on the next flight back to D.C. You don't belong here. You're not right for him anymore." His lips pressed into a thin line and his eyes darkened into twin lumps of coal. "You're a liability and Ryker doesn't need any distractions right now. He owes me."

Pain rippled through my chest, and I struggled for my next breath. "What's that supposed to mean?"

His smile turned reptilian. "We made a deal. I helped him rescue you, and now he has to help me."

I circled my arms around my waist, trying to hold myself together. My nerve endings prickled. "Help you with what?"

Ignacio angled his head to the side. "Rever's gone. I needed a new successor. Now I have one."

My hands shook as I threw the sheets off my body. I bolted out of the bed like it was on fire. It took all my power not to wrap my hands around his neck and strangle the life from his body. I dug my fingernails into the palms of my hands until I mentally winced.

"You're lying," I hissed. "He would never agree to that. He doesn't want anything to do with your perverse cartel. He doesn't want anything to do with you. He promised me." My voice fractured on the last word, making me sound pathetic. Weak. Vulnerable. At that moment, I was all of those and worse.

Ignacio rolled his eyes. "For God's sake, Miss Covington. Grow up. That's exactly what he did, and you don't have anyone but yourself to blame. You did this to him. You shouldn't have left that hotel. You shouldn't have come back to Mexico."

A rush of saliva flooded my mouth, and nausea rolled through me as the last three months finally caught up with me.

Lies.

Betrayals.

Secrets.

Fear.

My pregnancy.

Being taken as a hostage.

Now this...Ryker had pledged his future to the Vargas Cartel. No wonder he had fought me every step last night. He was going to push me out of his life. It was only a matter of hours, and I'd be alone again in a prison of my making, but this time I'd have a child. A hurricane of sadness slammed into my chest.

"Please," I begged as an unhinged sob sloshed out of my mouth. "Please don't force him do this. He doesn't want it. You're going to kill him."

"It's already done. He gave me his word. You know him well enough to know his word means everything."

What about his promises to me? Did they mean less than his promises to Ignacio?

Every time I thought I'd made progress and put the past behind me, life punched me in the face. I couldn't take anymore. The last thread of the rope tethering me to reality severed. All of my disjointed emotions twisted like a tornado inside my gut.

Suffocated by his betrayal, I couldn't breathe. I couldn't form a coherent sentence. My limbs trembled like branches in a windstorm. With one hand, I clutched my chest trying to calm the frenetic beat of my heart. With the other, I reached for the headboard to brace my weight, but I didn't move fast enough. The room swirled before my eyes in a blur of jewel tones and surprised faces.

Pain vibrated up my knees, and my head snapped forward, crashing into the tiled floor. Blood burst from my nose, and streamed down my face. A shower of white stars flickered behind my eyes. I licked my lower lip, and the warm metallic taste of copper coated my tongue.

A hand stroked the back my head. Two sets of dark eyes searched mine. Two mouths moved open and closed. Shouts and rapid-fire questions echoed through my ears, but I couldn't understand anything. I didn't want to. It was too hard. I didn't want to fight any longer. My emotions turned off like a spigot. Numbness slithered through my veins like a lethal injection. I felt so heavy.

Too heavy.

Too tired.

Worn out.

Just like that my eyes slid closed, and I embraced the darkness. I invited it in, and willed it to claim me. Giving up had never felt so peaceful.

Chapter Fourteen

Ryker

"She fainted?" I squeezed my phone against my ear as I ran up the front steps of the Vargas compound. "How the hell did that happen?"

"Calm down," Emanuel said. "Dr. Mendez took care of her. She's resting in your room."

"Is he still there?"

"No, he left, but you can call him if you have any questions."

I pressed the code to unlock the front door and flung it open the minute the light flashed green. "I'm here. Where's Ignacio?"

Emanuel sauntered around the corner and slipped his phone into his pocket. "He went to his room to rest. He wasn't feeling well. He's still not one hundred percent."

"Did he do something to upset Hattie?"

Emanuel rubbed the back of his neck as he glanced to the side. "I don't think he *did* anything to her."

Anger vibrated through my nerve endings. "But

he said something, right?"

"Apparently, he told her you intended to stay in Mexico and work with Ignacio."

"What the fuck? Why would he do that?"

He shrugged. "How the hell am I supposed to know? I wasn't there. It probably came up in conversation. It's not like he lied to her. He told her the truth. She didn't like it. She fainted."

"I wanted her to hear it from me," I growled.

"Then you should've told her this morning instead of hiding your head in the sand."

I pointed my finger at him. "You don't know what you're talking about. Shut the fuck up."

Smirking, he raised one eyebrow. "Or what?"

I shoved him in the shoulder. "Get out of my face or I'll take this up with Ignacio."

"Oh please." He snorted. "Ignacio listens to me. He trusts me. Look what happened with Rever."

"What are you talking about?" I spat.

"I discredited him."

"He did it to himself."

He chuckled. "Maybe so, but I gave him the push he needed. He's not that smart. I planted ideas in his head, and he took the bait." He shrugged. "Then lo and behold, Ignacio started doubting him, pushing him, and he spiraled in a mess of his own making. Now he's holed up in some shithole in Panama with that Alvarez whore."

I didn't think. I lunged for him. My hand curled into his shirt, and I pinned him against the wall. His head whipped backward, crashing into the wall like a rag doll. The heel of my hand pressed against his windpipe. His eyes bulged. I wanted to kill him. I was so sick of this shit. I didn't want anything to do with Ignacio, Emanuel, or the Vargas Cartel.

"You think you're smart enough to manipulate me?"

"I know I am," he croaked.

"You don't know anything."

He spat on my face. Saliva dripped down my cheek. "I got rid of Rever and I'll get rid of you too if I feel like it. You think Ignacio's in control, but he's not. I call all the shots."

Poison laced laughter exploded from my mouth. "What happened to all that sanctimonious bullshit about not wanting to lead the cartel and being happy with your lot in life?"

"I could wrestle control from Ignacio in a second if I wanted to." He snapped his fingers. "That should tell you something."

I slammed his body against the wall. "That I'd be doing Ignacio a favor if I killed you."

"Rever was too impulsive, and I'm starting to think you're not much better."

My fist had a mind of its own. It landed in the dead center of his right cheek. His head jerked to the side. Fire shot up my arm, and my knuckles buckled, but I didn't care. I welcomed the pain.

"Listen," I hissed through clenched teeth. "I don't give a shit about the Vargas Cartel or Ignacio's legacy. You can have the cartel. I don't want anything to do with it, but don't play mind games with me. You won't win."

The veins on the side of his neck bulged, and his jaw muscle ticked. "Is that a challenge?"

"Make what you want of it. All I ask is that you

stay far away from Hattie and me. When it comes to either of us, keep your opinions to yourself." I shoved him to the side. "Now get the fuck away from me before I change my mind."

Emanuel ran his hand down the side of his swollen cheek. "Ignacio won't like this."

Smirking, I raised one eyebrow. "What gave you the impression I give a shit what Ignacio does or doesn't like?"

"What won't I like?" Ignacio said as he strolled into the room.

"I thought you were sleeping," Emanuel said, his eyes boring into the wall above Ignacio's head.

Ignacio leaned his shoulder into the wall, his narrowed eyes boomeranging between Emanuel and me. "How could I sleep with this noise? Now are either of you going to tell me what the hell is going on or do we have to play twenty questions?"

I stuffed my swollen hand in my pocket. Not that it'd conceal what happened. Emanuel's face looked like he had a third eye growing out of his cheek. "We had a disagreement."

"A disagreement that ended with your fist in his face," he said wearily.

I glared at Ignacio. "Something like that."

He scowled for a second, then his hardened stare cut to Emanuel. "Do you have something to add or did you suddenly become mute?"

Emanuel folded his arms across his chest and drummed his fingers against his biceps. "It was a misunderstanding, but we're good now."

"Is that right, Ryker?" Ignacio asked.

"I don't trust him." Ignacio sliced his hand

through the air in front of him, interrupting me. "No," I said, shaking my head. "I know you trust him, and I know he's worked for you for a long time, but that doesn't mean I should trust him with my interests. With the people I care about. I don't think you should either."

Emanuel scoffed. "Your cryptic bullshit doesn't make sense. I know you have a long résumé back in the States, but you don't know anything about the way things work in Mexico."

"And you just proved my point." I pinned Ignacio with my eyes. "He's trying to undermine me just like he undermined Rever."

Emanuel chuckled. "You don't need me to do it. You're doing a good job all by yourself."

"What's that supposed to mean?"

"Juan Alvarez is alive. You killed his son. You helped kidnap his daughter. If you intended to escalate the war between the two cartels, you succeeded. This whole mess is going to get a hell of a lot bloodier before it's put to rest."

Ignacio's mouth tugged down in a disapproving frown, and he scrubbed his hand down his face. "I don't have time to mediate this pissing contest right now. What's done is done. As for Juan, we'll figure out how to deal with him later. He's a sick fuck, but he can't do anything from his hospital bed. We still have time to come up with a plan."

I clenched my hands. "But you had time to spill all my secrets to Hattie," I said bitterly.

Ignacio rolled his eyes and blew out an exaggerated breath. "So what? I ripped the bandage off. It had to be done. You were dragging your feet.

You and I both know she doesn't belong here. The quicker you sever your connection with her, the quicker you'll learn what you need to know to help me."

I took a deep breath, struggling to maintain control. "I didn't need your help with Hattie. I had everything under control until you opened your mouth."

Ignacio raised one brow. "Really?"

"I planned to talk to her tonight," I said through gritted teeth. Less than a week with the Vargas Cartel, and I was already losing my sanity. It was like living in a den of poisonous snakes. I couldn't trust anyone. Not even my own father.

Ignacio stuffed his hands in his pockets. "Then, take care of it. I heard she's awake now. The last time I checked, your friend Noah was in there with her."

"He's not my friend. I hardly know him."

"Well, Hattie seems to like him. Maybe he'd be willing to take her off your hands."

Ignacio intended to piss me off. I knew it. He knew it. Unfortunately, the knowledge that he wanted to provoke me didn't stop the anger from swirling in my gut like the flames of hell.

"Yeah, well, unlike you, I don't make other people do my dirty work."

Ignacio's eyes narrowed. "What's that supposed to mean?"

"You're smart enough to put the pieces together. Figure it out," I said as I stalked down the hallway.

I had agreed to Ignacio's terms, but I couldn't go through it. It was like all the pieces finally slid into place. I wasn't going to bend to Ignacio's will. I made a bargain with him. I gave him my word, but he owed Hattie. He owed me. I considered my debt to him paid in full. Right then, I promised myself, I'd find a way out of the Vargas Cartel's web or die trying. Life was too short to let Hattie slip through my fingers. If I lost her, then I didn't have any reason to live. I understood that now.

I needed to fix the mess I'd made. Plain and simple. I promised I'd take care of Hattie, and for some reason, I'd convinced myself that meant pushing her out of my life forever. That might've been true on some level, but deep down I knew I wanted and needed her more than anything or anyone. As a kid, I learned if I wanted something I had to fight for it and never give up. In the midst of this whole debacle with Ignacio, I'd forgotten that, but that would change starting right now.

Chapter Fifteen

Hattie

"What the hell are you doing in here?" Ryker roared the minute he walked into the room. The door thudded against the doorstop.

I slowly lifted my gaze from the creamy sheets covering my legs. I'd been drawing circles on the individual threads for the last twenty minutes as I explained bits and pieces of my situation to Noah. I didn't understand why I decided to unload on him. He'd helped me last night without comment or judgment, and something about his compelling caramel colored eyes convinced me to confide in him.

Noah leaned back against the headboard and propped his hands behind his head. His leg brushed against my thigh. Ryker's gaze laser focused on the brief contact, and his jaw clenched.

"You're full of sunshine today," Noah said.

"I asked you a question."

Noah patted me on my leg, and I turned to look at him. Really look at him. He was cute. No, cute was an understatement. He was downright sexy. He had dark hair, exotic hooded eyes framed by heavy lashes, and lips perpetually curved up at the corners. If my heart hadn't chained itself irrevocably to Ryker months ago, my stomach might have flipped every time his gaze landed on me. As luck would have it, I felt nothing except a detached appreciation like I was admiring a designer handbag or a beautiful sculpture.

"I'm checking in on our girl. I wanted to make sure she was feeling better. She was pretty out of it when I helped her to bed last night," Noah answered, a huge smile spreading across his face.

Ryker's vein ticked in his neck like a time bomb waiting to go off. "Well, you can leave now. I'm sure you have somewhere to be."

Noah shot me a sideways glance and winked. "I don't actually. Hattie was just telling me how she wanted to fly backing to the States tomorrow. She needs to find a place to live and get caught up on some requirements to finish her degree. I have some business to take care of in D.C., so I agreed to accompany her and help her get settled. That is, if you're too busy?"

Ryker's hands flexed. "You're leaving?" he barked, his words hanging in the air with the weight of a storm gathering on the horizon.

"That's the plan," I replied. I kept my voice empty of emotion, painstakingly ignoring the leaden weight ballooning in the pit of my stomach.

His forehead scrunched. "You weren't going to discuss this with me first."

I blinked away the urge to cry. Since the doctor

left two hours ago, I'd been on an emotional rollercoaster. "Noah, can you give us some space? Ryker and I need to talk."

"Sure," he said, clearing his throat. "I'll be around here all day if you want to finish our conversation." He kissed me on the top of my head and jumped out of the bed. I could still smell a whiff of sandalwood as I watched him disappear down the hallway.

Ryker settled into a chair in the corner of the room, his long legs bent at a ninety-degree angle. He propped his elbows on this knees and knitted his fingers together. His shirt pulled against his wide shoulders. Lines bracketed his mouth. Even vibrating with anger, his graceful movements drew me to him like a magnet. I couldn't look away. Somehow, he magically soothed and unnerved me at the same time.

"Do you want to tell me what's going on?" His voice dropped a fraction. "Why you're trying to run away without talking to me?"

If I weren't so frustrated with him, I would feel guilty about considering Noah's offer to accompany me back to D.C., but given Ignacio's revelations I refused to second-guess my actions. Ryker's feelings were the least of my problems. I had to pull my life together and figure out how I was going to raise a kid alone. Ignacio didn't come out and say Ryker planned to kick me out of his life, but I knew it was only a matter of days. The writing was on the wall last night, but I'd been too blinded by my need for him to see the truth.

I didn't doubt Ryker's love for me. He would've

let me rot in that shitty house with the Alvarez Cartel if didn't love me. Instead, he sacrificed his future for me. But even knowing all that, I was paralyzed at the thought of moving forward without him. Once again, my future had been ripped out from underneath me, and I was damn sick of it.

I shrugged. "Why don't you go first? You're the one that's been keeping secrets."

Shadows flickered across his face, and his sooty hued eyes looked right through me. "Do you feel well enough to go for a walk around the grounds?" he countered.

My brows pinched together. "Apparently, I'm a prisoner here. Ignacio told me I wasn't allowed to go anywhere."

The corners of his lips twitched, and my heart stuttered. Damn his flirty lips. Damn his sinful eyes. Damn my heart for wanting him so much.

"Alone," he clarified. "I didn't want you going anywhere alone." He paused and his smiled widened. Hot, tangled sensations danced down my spine. "Besides, I'd like some privacy. I don't want to add to Ignacio's video collection or have him overhear us."

Heat rushed to my face as last night flashed through my mind. "Oh my God," I said, bile swirling in my gut in spite of the anti-nausea medicine the doctor gave me. I didn't want to add to the stockpile of blackmail material Ignacio had of me. One video was enough. I trusted Ryker, but I would never trust Ignacio. "Not again."

His smile softened, and he peered at me lazily, his eyes hooded. "Don't worry. I deleted it this morning before anyone woke up. Nobody will ever see it, but I have some stuff I want to talk to you about without worrying that we'll be overheard."

He didn't have to ask me twice. I wanted to talk to him without prying ears and eyes. I scooted off the bed and tugged on the hem of the t-shirt Ryker gave me last night. "I need clothes," I announced, waving my hand in front of my body.

An amused laugh erupted from his mouth, and he pointed to a white paper bag on the floor next to his dresser. "The housekeeper is washing the clothes you left at the hotel. There's a dress, panties, and other necessities in there."

"I wish somebody would've pointed that out earlier," I grumbled as my bare feet padded against the tiled floor. I'd been hiding in bed the entire day due to a lack of proper clothing.

I found a simple light blue shift dress with iolite trim and white lacy panties in the bag. With my back turned to him, I took off the t-shirt and tossed it on the top of the dresser. I slipped the dress over my head and pulled on the panties.

I still hadn't looked in the mirror. I avoided it like the plague last night in the bathroom, but a quick brush of my hand over my face told me all I needed to know. One of my cheeks was still slightly swollen, my lower lip was cracked, and my hand looked like I had smashed it between two bricks. At least Dr. Mendez bandaged the burns on my upper arm. I couldn't stand to look at them.

I spun around and finger combed my hair. "I'm ready. Where to?"

Ryker stood less than a foot away from me. He

tucked a strand of hair behind my ear. His familiar spicy sea scent washed over me. "I'm sorry I left before you woke up. I should've told you everything last night. I shouldn't have left you alone with Ignacio."

His apology ignited sparks of anger in my blood, and I curled my fingernails into my palms like razors. "After everything I've been through, I can't believe you abandoned me like that. You didn't even stay around long enough for the doctor's exam. If you really go through with whatever fucked up plan you have in your head—"

"Hattie, listen to me," he interrupted.

"No. I know you think you're going to make some bullshit noble sacrifice and push me out of your life. But if you do go through with it, it's over. I will never let you back in my life. You will never know anything about our child. You will never know his name. You will never see his face. We will disappear. Do you understand what I'm saying? This is your last chance. Don't fuck it up."

Ryker pulled me into his arms, and his warm, minty breath shuffled through the ends of my hair. The heat from his touch bled through the gauzy fabric of my dress. My pulse skyrocketed, and a shiver of anticipation danced down my spine. I should've pushed him away, but I didn't. I couldn't. I never could think clearly when it came to Ryker.

He was my weakness.

My Achilles heel.

My kryptonite.

My everything.

"Hattie, I am so sorry about everything that

happened to you. You have no idea how badly I wish I could go back in time and make different decisions." He squeezed me tighter and I could barely breathe. "I'm not going to lie. The thought crossed my mind that you'd be better without me. I still think so. It's not too late to rebuild your life. I would make sure you had enough money to buy a house, finish your degree or stay home with our baby if that's what you wanted. I would make it so you never wanted for anything."

Alarm zipped through my body like a lightning bolt, and a monster sized black hole opened up inside of my chest.

"Except you." My voice was tight with suppressed tears. "Is loyalty to your father more important to you than your unborn child or me?" I slipped my hands between our bodies and shoved him, but he didn't move.

"Fuck no, Hattie. That's crazy." He buried his nose in my hair and inhaled. "You mean everything. That's the only reason I considered leaving you. I didn't know what to do. I needed to think. I needed a plan."

I tipped up my head, pinning him with my eyes. "And you have one now?"

Silence ticked by, and I bit my lip, wishing I felt stronger, more confident. Instead, I wilted under his unreadable gaze. He exhaled and took a couple of steps back, his hands slipping from my shoulders. I immediately mourned the loss of his touch. Guilt etched lines into his face as he ran a hand through his inky hair. His normally vibrant gray eyes were stormy.

"I have ideas, but I'll need your help. We'll need to work together," he said, his voice low and cautious.

I rubbed my hands over my face and my throat constricted. My head pounded, and sadness poured through my veins like a drug making me tired and weak. "I don't know how I can help. I'm kind of out of my depth here."

"Come on. Let's take a walk." The pads of his fingers whispered like silk down my arm, and he laced his fingers through mine.

I hesitated for a moment. A small sliver of me wanted to flee this whole mess, but I didn't think it'd do any good. I had to trust Ryker to guide us through this just like he had with everything else we had faced. Despite all the ups and downs, he hadn't failed me yet.

"Okay." I said, my lips trembling. I swallowed hard, struggling to swallow the sadness and fear creeping up the walls of my throat.

His lips quirked up, and he kissed the tip of my nose. "We've got this, Hattie. We're going to fix this." I stared into his eyes and drank in his too sexy smile. "I love you. You're safe. I'm safe. The baby's safe now, and I'm going to do everything to keep it that way. That's all that matters."

Chapter Sixteen

Ryker

I closed the door behind us and wandered to the pool with Hattie. I hated summer in the Yucatan. The wet air licked every exposed inch of skin, and the sun felt close enough to touch, almost like standing next to a brick oven. Each step outside was like drudging through a steam shower fully clothed.

"Are you going to start this conversation or are you waiting for me?" Hattie asked as we circled the pool for the second time.

I halted mid-stride near the tree line framing the edge of the pool area. I tipped up my head, squinting at the bright blue sky above us. The birds chirped. The bees buzzed. The jets in the pool hummed. A rare breeze shuffled her hair, and individual strands danced around her face like flames. The scent of chlorine tickled my nose, but I froze. Every time I opened my mouth, the words wouldn't come out. I didn't know where to begin. My mind was as blank as the day I was born. Words were my enemy.

She squeezed my hand tighter, and I found the courage to move forward. I cleared my throat. "Let's sit here," I said, pointing to the bench beneath a row of palm trees.

Her eyes searched my face, and the corners of her lips turned down. "Just say what you need to say. You're scaring me."

I rubbed my free hand down the side of my face. "You have to go home. The sooner, the better. Maybe I could find a flight for you tonight, but no later than tomorrow morning," I blurted out.

"No."

I arched a brow. "It's non-negotiable."

She ripped her hand out of my grasp and straightened the hem of her dress. "Wait. I'm confused. We're back to that?" Betrayal bled from her words. "I can't believe this. All those pretty words and promises you fed me a few minutes ago were nothing more than a pile of meaningless syllables strung together to appease me. I don't get. Why'd you bother?"

I rubbed my palms along the sides of my thighs. "Hold on, Hattie. You're jumping to conclusions. It's not what you think."

She pressed her hand to her chest like she wanted to stop her heart from breaking. "Then tell me what I should be thinking right now because all I'm hearing is that you want me out of your life as soon as possible. I can't believe that after everything we've been through, you're ready to throw us away without fighting for us. For me. For our baby." She shook her head and sucked in a few monster breaths. She tried to act strong, but I heard the tremor in her voice. I hated hurting her.

"Okay. Okay," I said, holding up my hands in mock surrender. "Let's start from the beginning. I'm not trying to throw anything away."

"You thought about it. You admitted it," she accused, her voice laced with contempt.

"My main concern is your safety, and if sacrificing our relationship is the *only* way to keep you safe, then I will do it."

Sadness haunted her face, and she closed her eyes for a beat. "So that's it? You made up your mind," she said, her lips trembling.

"No." I dragged a hand through my hair. "If you still want me, I'm going to fight for us."

She sighed, and her brows lifted, prompting me to continue. "Okay. That's what I wanted to hear. That's how you should've started this conversation."

I laughed. "Good to know."

She perched on the edge of the gray concrete bench and crossed her ankles. "Go ahead and explain what you're thinking."

With my hands deep in my front pockets, I paced back and forth in front of her for a few seconds, considering my words. Then I crouched down in front of her. "Ignacio already told you I agreed to help him with the cartel if he helped me rescue you."

She angled her chin to the side, and her eyes narrowed a fraction of an inch. "Ignacio said as much, but I didn't know whether I should believe him. I don't trust him."

"It's the truth. He's planning to groom me to be

his successor."

She dropped her head into her hands, and a fractured breath wheezed through her lips. "Oh God, Ryker. Why would you agree to that? What were you thinking?"

I gently brushed the hair away from her face. "I was thinking about you. I didn't have any options, and there was no way in hell I would let you rot in that safe house begging for Juan Alvarez's mercy while I came up with an alternative."

"I appreciate what you did, but you don't want this." She puckered her lips, and her cheeks hollowed. "You hate this place. You hate everything the Vargas Cartel stands for."

I squeezed her knee. "You're right. I do, but it was the only thing I had to offer Ignacio."

"So what now?"

"I need you to leave. I don't want Ignacio or anyone else to use you as leverage against me. When this is over, I'll find you." I curled my hands into the hem of her dress, struggling to calm my racing heart. The thought of either Ignacio or that piece shit Juan Alvarez getting near Hattie or threatening her made me crazy.

Her head shook back and forth and strands of her brown whipped in front of her face. "No. Absolutely not. It's not happening. Don't even try to force to me leave. You've already done that once."

"Why not?" I grumbled.

Her entire body tensed. "I won't be any safer there than I would be with you. In fact, I think I'll be in more danger. I'll be a sitting target for any of your enemies and the Deverons."

I rested my head on her knees for a minute gathering my thoughts. She was right. We had so many enemies.

Ignacio.

Juan Alvarez.

Senator Deveron.

Evan Deveron.

Emanuel.

And those were just the ones I knew about. As more people got wind of my connection to the Vargas Cartel, I'd have enough enemies to fill a ballroom.

"I think you need to deal with Senator Deveron and Evan and I'll find a way to make sense of Ignacio and Juan Alvarez."

"What do you mean deal with Senator Deveron and Evan?"

I sat on the bench next to her. "We need to expose their connection to the cartel. Then, they'll be discredited or worse. Senator Deveron won't have any power to hurt you anymore, and you won't have to worry about Evan."

"And how are we going to do that?"

He rubbed his lips together. "You'll leak information and evidence corroborating the connection to any newspaper or website that will listen." I'd have to search Ignacio's office, which wouldn't be easy, but I'd find a way to do it without alerting him. I needed at least a week to put the rest of my plan in motion before Ignacio discovered my deception.

Hattie didn't move or speak for a few drawn out

seconds. "And you want me to go back to D.C. to do it."

My chest tightened. I didn't want her to go anywhere. I wanted to chain her to my side forever, and never let go. "Yes. I think it's the smartest way to get this done," I said instead.

She closed her eyes and bowed her head, even as her hands fidgeted in her lap. "And you won't come with me?"

"No. I need to stay here and take care of Ignacio and Juan."

Hattie stilled, and her eyes blinked open, wide and alarmed. "I can't do it alone."

"I know. I was planning to send Noah with you," I said quietly.

The words tasted like ash in my mouth, and something inside of me splintered. I didn't want Noah anywhere near her. I saw the way he looked at her this morning. He wanted her, but I trusted her, and I hoped to hell it wasn't misplaced. Either way, she deserved to be happy regardless of who made that happen. My lips twisted in perfect synchronicity with my gut at the thought. I shook my head, trying to eradicate the jealousy from my mind. The jealousy could wait. The rest of this mess wouldn't.

"Who will help you?"

"Don't worry about me." I placed my hand on her lower belly, and she pulled her bottom lip through her front teeth. "Just take care of yourself and our baby, and I'll find you when this is done."

She leaned her head against my shoulder, gazing at me. Tears shimmered in her golden eyes. "You promise?" she said quietly, her voice breaking on the last word.

Our gazes held, and I smiled softly, my heart drumming hollowly in my chest. I slid my hands into the silky strands of her hair. "I promise. I wouldn't have it any other way."

It'd be damn hard to keep my promise. If Ignacio got wind of what I was planning, he'd kill me, but there was no turning back. She'd always be my soft spot. My enemies wouldn't hesitate to use her to get to me. I had to finish this once and for all. It was the only way I could guarantee Hattie's and our baby's safety. I understood that now. I had to eliminate them before they eliminated us.

Kill or be killed.

Destroy or be destroyed.

Attack or be attacked.

It wasn't even a question. No more waiting. We had to go on the offensive and wage our own war.

Chapter Seventeen

Hattie

I tossed and turned, chasing sleep, but my mind had other plans. Ryker had left me in his room over an hour ago while he went to search Ignacio's records. He told me to go to sleep, and I'd tried. I really did.

My mind circled relentlessly. My ears labored to hear every noise. My shoulder muscles crawled up the back of my neck. Minute after minute passed, and I swore I heard footsteps a million times, but nothing happened. No one came in the room. I finally gave up trying to sleep and turned on the lamp on the nightstand.

Just when I convinced myself Ryker was bleeding to death somewhere in the house, and I needed to go find him, the door handle dipped. I sat up in bed, clutching the sheets to my chest with one hand and fingering the gun Ryker gave me with the other. My irregular breaths echoed unnaturally in the room.

The door cracked open. A sliver of yellow light

spilled onto the creamy travertine tiled floor. Afraid to make a sound, I held my breath and stared as the yellow sliver grew, inch by painful inch. A silhouette shaded the opening. My heart rapid-fired inside my chest.

Thump.

Thump.

Thump.

At its current rate, my heart would explode by the time the door fully opened. The hinges squeaked. My breath hitched.

Please don't be Ignacio or worse…

"Hattie?" Ryker said, pausing in the entrance. "Is everything okay?"

I swallowed over the lump lodged in my throat. "Oh my God. You scared the crap out of me."

His dark eyebrows knitted together. "Did something happen while I was gone?"

I shook my head. "No. I couldn't sleep. I was worried about you."

He closed the door behind him. "You should be sleeping. Your flight leaves early in the morning." He leaned against the door with a wicked smile on his face. "But I can't say I'm sad you're awake."

"Why's that?"

"Because now I can kiss you goodnight."

I rolled my eyes. "Did you find anything we can use?"

He tapped a large yellow envelope against his leg, and his lips pinched together until they almost disappeared entirely. "I found more than enough." He held up the envelope. "Everything you need is in here. Don't look at it until you get back to the States with Noah."

I frowned. "I can't read it on the plane?"

"No." He unzipped my suitcase and emptied out my clothes.

I tossed the sheets to the side, and I jumped out of the bed. "What are you doing?"

"I'm hiding this," he answered without looking at me.

I looked at him askance. "I can put it in my purse."

"This is better." He pulled a switchblade from his pocket and sliced open the silky black lining in the suitcase. He slipped the envelope inside and squirted a few dots of glue on the lining, temporarily sealing the cut.

I nodded. "What am I supposed to do with the information?"

He tapped me on the tip of my nose. "Noah knows what to do. He'll talk to you about it on the plane."

"When did you talk to him?"

His eyes turned serious, but a faint smile remained on his face. "Just now."

"Oh." I sat on the edge of the bed. "Why do I need to go with him? If he's taking the lead, I can stay with you. I want to be here to support you."

He sighed as he settled onto the bed next to me, his hand weaving around my waist. His soft touch seared my side, his thigh leaning into mine, and his long fingers flexing into my skin.

"It's better that way," he said, his voice heavy with emotion. "I don't know what will happen here. There are so many moving pieces and things I can't control. If you leave, it's one less thing I need to worry about."

"Yeah. You're probably right," I said softly, even as a dull ache burrowed under my breastbone. As much as I wanted to glue myself to Ryker's side, I sure as hell didn't want to end up chained to a wall again because he couldn't protect me.

My nerves were shot from straining to catch every sound over the last two hours, and my exhaustion made me jittery. Ryker slid his arm up my back to my shoulders and I buried my head into his chest, seeking strength in his embrace. I promised myself I would stay strong and not cry until I was safe at home, but I fell apart. Tears burned behind my eyes, and a strangled sob fled my mouth as I exhaled.

"Shh, it's okay," he whispered next to my ear.

I tried to stand up, but he pulled me back down next to him.

"How long do you think?" I asked. My words were muffled from pressing my face into his chest, trying to capture every last molecule of his scent and sear it into my memory.

He kissed the top of my head. "Not long. A couple of weeks. Maybe a month if things get really complicated."

I lifted my head even though I felt empty with defeat. My heart felt like it was made of glass, ready to shatter at the slightest touch. "Not a month. You can't leave me for that long. I'll be showing by then, and everybody will know. What will I say? What will I do?"

What everyone thought of me should've been the

least of my concerns, but it wasn't. My mom would lose her mind. My dad would say nothing as usual, but he wouldn't have to. He communicated his disapproval with silence rather than words. My mom and dad made a good team in that respect. She said everything he wouldn't and he sealed the deal by pretending I didn't exist. His arm slid from my shoulder and I shivered.

"I didn't want to do this yet." He kneeled in front of me and tilted his head to the side. "Well, that's not true. I planned to do it right when we got to Mexico, but everything was strained and then it fell apart."

I nodded, unable to mutter a single word. He slipped his hand into his pocket, pulled out a black velvet box, and cracked it open. There was a large diamond solitaire framed by so many tiny diamonds it looked like a starburst. I cupped my hand over my mouth, unsure whether I wanted to laugh or cry. Maybe both.

"This isn't how I planned to ask you to marry me. I wanted this moment to be perfect and filled with promises of a beautiful future. I wanted you to be happy. I wanted to surprise you—"

"Mission accomplished. You did surprise me," I whispered, the words barely audible over the swish of the ceiling fan and the leaping of my heart in my chest. "I wasn't expecting this. I never thought that far ahead. There was always so much going on. There was so much to figure out…" Realizing I was rambling, my voice faded to nothing.

His knuckles brushed along my face, and I felt his touch all the way down to my toes. "I know and just to be clear I don't want you to say yes right now." He pinned me with his gray eyes, an endearing, almost boyish, smile on his face. "It's still not the right time, but I want to give you this ring so you'll know where my heart is even if things get ugly and complicated."

My lips trembled, and endless tears poured down my face, but I didn't care. I wanted him to see how much this moment meant to me even if I couldn't find the perfect words. "Things have been that way between us since the beginning, but that didn't stop us before. It won't stop us now."

He nodded as he fingered the diamond ring inside the box. It sparkled in the dim room as the light hit the delicate angles of the stone. "Yeah." He smiled faintly, his eyes glowing with an intensity that made my heart sputter. "You're right, and I have a feeling things are going to get a lot worse before they get better, but you're worth it." He swallowed hard. "I'd do anything for you. You know that, right?"

"I do."

He nodded. "This is going to be hard. You need to be strong. So many things could go—"

I held up my hand, interrupting him. I didn't want him to explain. If I understood all the hazards, I wouldn't be able to get out of bed tomorrow much less put the pieces in motion to destroy Senator Deveron and Evan. I needed to stay firmly focused on the end goal, not all the crap in between.

"I know, but I don't want to spend our last night together talking about all the bad stuff that could happen. I want to pretend like it doesn't exist." I licked my lips. "Just for tonight."

"Okay. I can do that." He slipped the ring out of the box and held it up between us like a peace offering. "When you look at this, I want you to remember that we're both working for the same goal."

"And what's that?" I asked, wanting to make absolutely sure we were on the same page. There wasn't any room for misunderstandings. We had to be in sync to make our plans work.

He laughed softly. "A lifetime together. I want to marry you and wake up every morning next to you. I want to celebrate every holiday, triumph, and birthday with you. I want to hold your hand through every hurt, tragedy, or moment of uncertainty." He squeezed my hand and pressed it against the center of his chest. "You are my heart. You are my soul. You are the best thing that ever happened to me."

His deep voice wrapped around my body like the softest blanket, and a cry of happiness escaped my mouth. He lifted my left hand and twirled the ring in front of me. His dark hair shone in the lamplight. His gray eyes glowed, drinking in every detail of my reaction.

"Can I put it on you?" he asked.

My breath snagged in my throat. "Yes. Oh my God. Yes." He guided the ring up my finger and I held it up, wiggling my fingers. "It fits," I whispered, feeling like Cinderella with the glass slipper.

"I love you, Hattie," he answered simply as he pressed a kiss to my parted lips. "Somehow we're going to make a life together. I don't know what it'll look like when everything unravels, but I do know it will be you, me, and our baby." He rested his hand on my lower belly, and his eyes reminded me of a lake at twilight—deep and endless, just like our love. "Every time you look at this ring remember that no matter how bad things get, we have each other."

My heart swelled. He promised to make all my dreams come true. I ached to kiss him and touch him. I didn't have to wait long. Strong arms circled around me, his fiery heat engulfing me. I swayed into him, molding our bodies together. He smelled like soap and him. Perfection.

He brushed his lips across mine with a quiet but steady hunger. When my tongue slipped between his lips, he released a strangled moan and my mind blanked. Lust surged through my veins, hot and languid. Desire crackled in the air. I couldn't tear my eyes away from his.

"I love you too," I whispered against his mouth, my voice thick and husky.

He leaned back, his eyes simmering with heat as his gaze trailed down my body and back up again.

"I'm so lucky you're mine," he said, his voice low and gruff. He gripped the back of my neck, crushing his lips against mine. Within seconds, the kiss exploded. His mouth was urgent, hot and persistent against mine. He tasted like earthy tequila, salt, and raw need. We only kissed for a brief moment, but it felt like forever as my worries slipped away and impatience to have him again squeezed around my chest. Breaking off the kiss, Ryker yanked my t-shirt over my head. His heavy-lidded eyes and slightly crooked smile set me on fire.

"Ryker," I whispered, my voice feather soft.

His fingers traced a line from my collarbone down the middle of my chest, painting my skin with tiny goosebumps. He paused when he reached the top edge of my panties, and I blew out a shuddering breath. His thumb slid beneath my panties, teasing me with every swipe. One perfectly timed movement would set me off. He brushed a kiss below my belly button. Aching with need, a moan spilled from my mouth.

"I need you," I said, latching onto his belt. I unbuckled it and shoved his pants down his hips as he pulled his shirt over his head. I wanted to touch every inch of him, mark him so he wouldn't forget what we meant to each other. "You really think it'll take a month?" I asked, thinking out loud as I nipped, bit, and licked his salty skin.

"God, I hope not," he hummed into my neck as he pushed me back on the bed. He licked the column of my throat, twisting his hands into my hair. I arched my head, giving him better access. My chest heaved, heavy breaths flowing like water from my mouth.

"Wait," I said, pushing him off me and sitting up again.

"What are you doing?"

"Shh," I said, sliding down onto my knees in front of him. I wrapped my hand around his thick erection. "I've never done this for you before and I want to. I need to taste you." I didn't know why I felt that way. I never felt that way before. Certainly not with Evan, but Ryker made me feel all kinds of new things. Things I didn't understand. Things I hadn't known. Things I hadn't even suspected.

He didn't say anything, but he didn't stop me.

"Fuck," he groaned as I licked the tip, drinking his salty taste. An answering heat rippled between my legs. "You don't have to do this."

I licked from the base to the tip. It was like warm velvet over steel on my tongue. "You don't like it?" I asked, looking at him through the fringe of my lashes. He looked down at me, and a lock of pitch-black hair fell in front of one of his eyes. I leaned forward and guided him inside of my mouth one inch at a time, my gaze never wavering from his face.

His nostrils flared, and his eyes fluttered closed. Harsh pants streamed from his mouth. The pulsing tension in his neck and the faint smile on his lips made my heart swell. I liked that I could bring him to the edge with my mouth.

"You know I do," he gritted out.

"So I shouldn't stop?"

His hands tangled in my hair, and he shook his head. "God, no," he said, his voice lowering an octave.

My hands skated up his thighs as I bobbed his length in and out of my mouth, gradually increasing my suction with every pass.

He tipped his head to the ceiling and groaned. His eyes were dark. "So close, Hattie. I'm so close."

"Mm," I hummed around his shaft, encouraging him to let go. I wanted to taste him. I moved faster.

In.

Out.

In.

"Stop," he growled. "This is so damn tempting, and don't get me wrong, I love your mouth on me, but I don't want to come like that tonight. Not if it's our last night."

He grabbed my arms, guided me onto the bed. Before I could utter a single word of protest, he spread my thighs and plunged deep inside of me. He was weighty, thick and hard. The air whooshed out of my lungs in one giant, involuntarily exhalation, almost as if my body wanted to exorcise everything from inside of me except him.

Then, he began to move in earnest and pleasure vibrated through my body with every thrust, drag, and circle. My nails dug into the ropes of muscle lining his shoulders. One of his hands tangled in my hair, and the other cupped my breast, pinning me to the mattress as though I'd leave if he didn't keep me tethered to the bed. Both primal and tender, his eyes devoured me. My insides contorted with love, and right then, I handed my heart to him and tossed the key in a bottomless abyss.

I countered every visceral flex of his hips with one of my own. Heated kisses showered my mouth and neck, turning me into ash. His sweaty chest licked mine in a choreographed erotic dance, and I never wanted it to end. If I could press the pause button and live in that moment forever, I would be tempted to do it.

My entire body shook as indescribable sensations spread through me multiplying with alarming speed, leaving no corner untouched or unmoved. My release turned and twisted, every muscle, ligament, and cell in my body tightening right down to my toes until I exploded. My vision blurred like I was drifting through a cloud and time fell away. A cry tore from my lips, and I arched into him, momentarily disrupting his rhythm.

His lips curled upward, and a chuckle mixed with a groan slipped from his parted lips. I dug my heels into the back of his thighs, pleading without words for him to keep going. Keep milking every ounce of pleasure from my body. Keep riding our connection until we're both boneless and satiated.

Ryker's shoulders tensed, and I whispered that I loved him, that I trusted him to keep me safe, and that I'd never stop fighting for us.

"I won't stop either," he promised, his voice guttural, his facial features fierce, resembling an ancient warrior. His hips jerked up, down, in and out with brutal force, possessing me, claiming me. Each jarring thrust of his pelvis against mine echoed through the room, sealing our promises. I loved it. I loved him. I would do whatever, fight whomever to keep him.

Moments later, a deep shudder ran through his body and then he collapsed on top of me. My limbs felt like liquid. Our chests pounded against each other almost as if our bodies were whispering silent promises to each other.

He started to roll off me, but I curled my hands around his upper arms. "No. Not yet," I muttered next to his ear. "I want to feel you next to me and inside of me as long as possible." I chuckled, recognizing the silliness in my words, but that didn't make them any less true. "Maybe we could sleep like this."

He nodded. "That sounds perfect to me," he admitted, his voice a soft rumble next to my ear. I let the words flow through my body like a rich glass of wine, savoring them, loving them.

Then, he bent his head, capturing my lips in a kiss that made me want to start all over again and celebrate our last hours together until neither of us could move. Without asking, he understood what I wanted. His hands roamed my body, grazing every inch as his tongue curled around mine. The twin rhythms of our breaths echoed in the room. Within a few minutes, his cock stirred to life inside of me, and we were right back where I wanted to be...forever.

Chapter Eighteen

Ryker

I pushed Hattie's hair away from her face and pressed a kiss to her trembling lips. "Are you ready to do this?"

She licked her lips. "As ready as I'll ever be."

I lifted her hand, slid the ring I gave her last night from her finger and placed it in her open palm. "Put this somewhere safe until you're on the airplane."

She slipped it in her pocket and closed her eyes. Her lashes cast shadows on her cheekbones. "Are you sure we have to do this?" A quiet desperation colored her words, turning my stomach inside out.

"Look at me," I whispered as I curled my hand around the side of her face. "It's just for show. Everything I say once we walk out this door doesn't mean anything."

Last night, we agreed to stage a fight so everyone believed we were no longer together. I didn't like the idea of the last words we'd share for weeks or longer being filled with hatred, but I needed to do everything possible to keep her safe. That meant explicitly showing everyone I didn't want her any longer.

"I know, but that doesn't mean it won't hurt," she said, her voice cracking.

"They're just words. Don't give them the power to hurt you. You know how I feel about you. What I say out there won't change anything."

I leaned in and kissed her one more time— maybe the last time if things exploded in my face. Her lips were soft and inviting. She tasted like mint and Hattie, the elixir of love and life. My tongue teased as it slid inside of her mouth, stoking my flame of never-ending desire for her. I tunneled my hands into her hair, deepening our kiss. A low moan slipped from her lips, and I swallowed it, burying it inside of me for later. I wanted to pull her into me. I wanted more time, but it wasn't possible. At least not today.

"Better?"

"Yes," she said quietly.

"I love you."

She smiled. "I love you, too."

I nodded and flung the door open.

"Get the fuck out of this house," I yelled as I stalked down the hall.

"Why are you doing this?" Hattie said, her voice small.

"Because we're over. You need to leave."

Her suitcase rumbled over the tile floor behind her as she followed me down the hall. "So that's it. After everything you put me through, don't you think you owe me a better explanation?"

I halted in the foyer by the front door. From the corner of my eyes, I saw Noah, Ignacio, and Emanuel sitting in the living room just as Noah and I agreed.

"Fuck, Hattie." I jerked my hand through the strands of my disheveled hair. "Do you want me to spell it out for you?"

She angled her chin to the side. "Yes."

"We had fun together. You were a good diversion, but I'm just not interested in you anymore. Being with you feels more like work than fun, and I don't want to work that hard."

She flinched, then her shoulders slouched. She looked so fucking defeated. I hated hurting her even if it wasn't real. I hated Ignacio. I hated the Vargas Cartel. I wished I could wrap her up in my arms and carry her away from this place. Instead, I dug my fingernails into my palms to stop myself from folding her into my arms.

"You said you loved me," she said, her voice trembling.

"I lied."

The color drained from her face. "What about the baby?"

I snorted as I whipped the front door open. "Oh please, Hattie. You don't even know if it's mine. It could be Evan's."

She stared at me for a long second, and my heart thudded wildly in my chest.

I love you. I love you. I love you. I willed her to see the truth in my eyes and stay strong.

"I guess you'll never know," she said softly.

"I guess not." I pulled her plane ticket from my

pocket and held it out in front of me. "Here."

"What's that?"

"A plane ticket. Noah is going to accompany you home to make sure I don't have to waste any more time or resources rescuing you again."

"Wow." A bitter laugh tumbled from her lips as she shook her head. "You really can't wait to get rid of me."

Noah crossed the room and wrapped his arm around her shoulder. He whispered something in her ear as he steered her toward the open door. I wanted to rip his lips off his face.

I folded my arms across my chest. "Go home, Hattie. Go back to Evan or whoever."

She whipped her head around, pinning me with her glassy eyes. "I fucking hate you. I wish I never met you. You ruined my life."

"Yeah, well, the feeling's mutual. Get her out of here, Noah."

She shrugged his arm off her shoulder. "I'm going. I don't need your lapdog to escort me out the door."

Then the door slammed shut, and she was gone.

"Ryker," Ignacio said as he walked across the room.

"I don't want to talk right now."

He patted me on the arm. "I know it doesn't seem like it now, but you did the right thing. Juan will go after her again. Sending her away is the only way she'll be safe."

I shrugged. "I was ready to move on."

Ignacio's brow furrowed. "What's that supposed to mean?"

My hands shook, and I shoved them into my pockets, hiding them. "I thought I loved her, but I don't. We're too different. We'd never work."

"What's going to happen with the baby?" Ignacio asked.

I rolled my shoulders, and I sucked in a breath through my nose. "I don't give a fuck," I hissed.

I didn't wait for his response. I needed to get away from him. I was going to be sick.

Chapter Nineteen

Hattie

I clutched the handle of my suitcase in one hand, dragging it behind me out of the automatic airport doors. It had been a long twenty-four hours, but now I was back in D.C. It didn't feel like home. It felt foreign. In fact, without Ryker I felt like a drifter clasping onto meaningless things that used to be the center of my world.

Taxis zipped in out of the parking lanes. Cars honked. Police officers directed traffic. Tourists and businessmen fumbled with their phones. Nothing about this felt right. I sucked in a deep breath, drawing the muggy air into my body. I'd spent so many years of my life being practical and making socially acceptable decisions, but every cell in my body begged me to turn around and run right back to Ryker. Frozen with indecision, I tapped my fingers on the hard plastic handle of my suitcase. I backtracked a few steps.

With his ear pressed to his cell phone, Noah glanced over his shoulder. "What the hell are you doing?" he mouthed.

My body sagged and I shook my head. "Nothing," I said. I had to stick with Ryker's plan. We needed to put all our ghosts to bed if we wanted to be together, and that meant eliminating the Deverons from my life permanently.

Frowning, he popped the trunk and loaded my luggage into the car. He didn't have anything except a small black bag. Then, he opened the back door of a black sedan and gestured for me to get in. He climbed in next to me, and the car pulled away from the curb.

"Do you have the papers?" he asked.

"Why?"

His heavily fringed eyes narrowed. "I need to review them before we walk into the meeting."

I folded my arms across my chest. "You're not coming in with me. I'm going to do this alone."

He angled his head to the side, and one side of his mouth curved up into a grin. "Yes. I am. Ryker wanted my help. I don't do things half-assed. I'm either all the way in or I won't bother."

"He wanted your help keeping me safe. Nothing else," I countered.

He squeezed my leg, and I scooted across the seat out of his reach. "He wanted my help with everything."

I drummed my fingers on the soft leather seat. "He didn't mention that to me. If he wanted you to see everything, he would've given you a copy or showed them to you last night."

"His mind was focused on other things."

"Like what?"

He stared at me wordlessly for a few seconds, his face inscrutable. "Warning me to keep my distance from you."

"What? Why the hell did he do that?" My mind swirled. Didn't he trust me?

Noah shrugged. "Who knows? I'm not privy to his inner thoughts, but you can call Ryker and talk to him about it." His lips twitched. "But he probably won't answer his phone. He can't risk anyone listening to his calls. For his plan to work, we need everyone to believe he severed all contact with you."

"I don't know if I should trust you." It wasn't entirely true. Since the moment he dragged me to the helicopter, he treated me with respect. He treated me like a friend, but being back in D.C. and knowing what we needed to accomplish, made me feel on edge. Part of me wanted to run to my dad with the evidence and beg him to help me, and wash my hands of the whole thing.

His eyebrows lifted in question. "Look, Hattie, Ryker asked for my help. He's paying me to help. In order to make this work, I need to know everything. I won't go into a mission blind."

I chewed on the inside of my cheek, debating what to do. "Fine," I conceded. "Tell me what you know and I'll fill in the blanks."

"Hattie," he said, drawing out my name, a mysterious smile toying with the corners of his lips. "Do you really think Ryker would send me here expecting you to keep me in the dark?" He glanced at his watch. "But if it makes you feel any better, I'll tell you what I know. We're meeting with the

D.C. Times in less than an hour. I know we will hand over evidence concerning Senator Deveron's ties to the Vargas Cartel if they agree to write the story."

"That sounds about right," I said.

"Good, so now you see why I'd like to see the papers before we give them to anyone else. They're going to be public soon enough anyway."

I sighed. He was right. "The papers are hidden in my luggage."

"Good." Smirking, he tugged on a strand of my hair. "We'll go over them at lunch and come up with a game plan."

Deciding I needed to tune everything out and relax for a few minutes, I snagged my ear buds and phone from my purse. I scrolled through my playlists and selected one I used when I couldn't sleep.

I glanced at Noah, and I noticed him eyeing me with one eyebrow raised.

I pulled out one of my ear buds. "What?"

He shook his head. "Nothing."

My brows slammed together and I shoved him playfully on his shoulder. "No. Tell me. I can practically hear the wheels in your head turning."

He surveyed me for a few seconds. "I just can't figure out why a girl like you is mixed up with a drug cartel thug. I understand how you met him, but that doesn't explain why you stuck around."

I jabbed a finger in the center of his center. "Ryker's not a drug cartel thug."

He chuckled. "Oh, he is. Don't try to deny it."

I folded my arms across my chest. "You don't

know anything about Ryker or me."

"Of course I do. You're Hattie Covington. Your father is the US Attorney General. Evan Deveron is your ex-fiancé. You are weeks away from getting your master's degree. You flaked on your internship at the Foreign Policy Council earlier this summer." He leaned back in the seat and crossed his ankles. "And for some reason, you're fixated on Ryker Vargas despite everything he and his family did to you." I held up my hand, but he ignored me. "Yes, I know the Vargas Cartel held you hostage, and I know why. It's not a secret. At least not with people who have connections."

Heat rushed to my face and my gut twisted. I opened my mouth to respond, but no words came out of my mouth. Honestly, I didn't have an explanation for my behavior. I didn't understand my feelings for Ryker. I knew I loved him. I knew he made my heart beat faster, my life spin a little quicker, but none of that was his business. I didn't owe him an explanation.

"Have I rendered you speechless?"

I huffed. "Just because you know a couple facts about my life doesn't mean you know me," I said, my voice raw and vulnerable. "Facts don't sum up a person."

He blinked, his eyes unreadable and then he ran a hand through his hair. "No, they don't, but you've got to admit your relationship with Ryker doesn't look so good on paper."

"You do realize if I listed a bunch of random facts about you, you wouldn't look so good either." I squared my shoulders and tapped a finger on my lips. "You're a mercenary for hire. People pay you to do bad things. You've killed people. You probably have more than one alias. Your loyalty only runs as deep as the pockets of the person paying you. Does that sound about right? Is that the sum of who you are, Noah? Or is there more to you than that?"

His nose flared, and then he shook his head, a cocky grin sliding across his face. "Touché, but that's none of your business."

I turned my head, holding his stare. "Then we agree on something. Don't judge me and I won't judge you."

"Agreed," he said.

I stuffed the ear bud back into my ear and closed my eyes. I hoped Ryker and I could wrap up this whole mess in less than a month.

Chapter Twenty

Ryker

Five days had passed since Hattie walked out of my life. I hadn't tried to call her, and she hadn't made any attempt to reach out to me. It was what we agreed, but it didn't mean I liked it. In fact, I hated it, but I was determined to protect her.

According to Noah, they hadn't made any progress in finding someone to feature the story about Senator Devcron's connection to Mexican drug cartels. Apparently, he managed to buy influence at more than a few new organizations over the last few years. In the end, it wouldn't matter. Somebody would cover the story and then it'd spread like an infectious disease. I just hoped it happened before Senator Deveron attempted to silence Hattie, but that was why I sent Noah with her.

I wasn't having any more luck than Noah and Hattie. My instincts told me Emanuel was the key to getting me out from under Ignacio's thumb. Regrettably, I hadn't uncovered much of anything about him. Either he had a pristine record of unwavering service to Ignacio and the Vargas Cartel, or he covered his tracks with diabolical precision. I believed it was the latter rather than the former.

My whole life I had pushed harder and harder until I succeeded and got what I wanted. This time wouldn't be any different. I had to keep my eyes open and have patience. Eventually, Emanuel would fuck up, and I'd be right there waiting for him.

I increased the incline on the treadmill, pushing myself to the limit, trying to forget everything for a few minutes and clear my mind. My feet pounded against the rubber track. Music blared from my ear buds. Sweat trickled down the side of my face and off my chin. My legs burned like I'd dipped them in fire, but I had no intention of stopping until physical exhaustion claimed my body. Maybe then, I'd have a chance of getting a decent night's sleep for the first time since Hattie left.

Someone yanked one of my ear buds out of my ear. "What?" I barked, slamming my hand on the stop button. My eyes collided with Rever's.

He lifted one eyebrow. "You've been calling me all week, but you haven't left a message."

I bent at the waist, cupping my knees as my chest heaved. "Why haven't you answered your phone?"

"I've been busy trying to start a new life away from this hellhole."

I pulled the other ear bud out of my ear, letting the cord dangle from the docking station. "Must be nice."

Rever's eyes drifted to the side. "Yeah, well, you're in luck. It didn't go too well so now I'm back."

My brows slammed together. "What's that supposed to mean?"

He stared at me in silence for a few seconds and then shrugged.

"Are you going to explain or should we play twenty questions?"

"Anna left me."

An involuntary laugh exploded from my lips. "I thought she was pregnant and you were going to get married."

He swore under his breath, running a hand down the side of his face. "So did I."

I took a long drink of my bottle of water. "So she's not pregnant."

"No."

Clutching, the handrails on the treadmill, I gritted my teeth. "You lied to me?"

A bitter laugh erupted from his lungs and he raked his hand through his hair. "No. She lied to me. I guess I'm as dumb as everyone believes."

"Why would she do that?"

"I don't know." He stuffed his hands into his pockets, his dark eyes stark. "We got into a fight. I left to give her some time to think, and she was gone when I came home in the morning."

"Maybe she'll come back."

"No." He shook his head. "She left a note." He pulled a balled up piece of paper from his pocket. "You want to read her parting words?"

I eyed the paper in his hand. "No, I'll pass, but

you can summarize them for me."

He glared at the paper and then he threw it across the room and into the trashcan. "Well, she flipped out when she found out you killed her brother, and her father was in the hospital. Things deteriorated from there."

I wiped a white hand towel over my face and swung it over my shoulder. "I can only imagine."

"It was a fucking mess. She threatened to leave me if I didn't help her family. Can you fucking believe it?" His lips twisted into a sneer. "She actually wanted me to rally behind Juan fucking Alvarez. There is no love lost between Ignacio and me, but I'd never betray him for Alvarez trash."

I raised my eyebrows. "Oh, really?" I mocked. "Because I'm pretty sure you already did when you stole his money to start a life with Anna *Alvarez*."

"Yeah, well, that was a mistake. She's a fucking bitch. She lied about everything. I don't even understand why. It doesn't make sense. I don't understand what she wanted to gain."

I picked up the television remote and turned up the volume as loud as it would go.

Rever waved his hand at the television. "What the hell is that about?" he shouted. I pointed to my ear, and then at the walls.

He nodded. "Got it."

"Will you spot me?" I asked as I stretched out on the charcoal weight bench. The angle of Rever's body would block my face from Ignacio's camera, and the loud volume would prevent anyone from hearing our conversation.

"Yeah."

"I think Emanuel set you up," I said as I lifted the weight bar. "I think he's collaborating with Juan Alvarez. Actually, I think he's been collaborating with him for a long time."

"Emanuel? Ignacio's ass kisser? Are we talking about the same person? He doesn't have a rebel bone in his body. He'd never do anything Ignacio didn't order."

"Yes," I ground out as I pushed the bar away from my chest. "We're talking about the same person, but you're wrong about him. He's a traitor. I think he initiated this whole war between Juan and Ignacio."

"You're crazy." Rever shook his head. "Emanuel's so far up Ignacio's ass, he'd never do anything like that. He's been working for Dad for a long fucking time."

"I know. Ignacio has reminded me on several occasions, but that's why it makes sense. Ignacio would never suspect him. He could get away with anything."

"I don't know, man."

"Think about it. He wanted you out of the picture. He made it happen. Then, all of a sudden I'm drawn back into the Vargas Cartel, but I don't think he has any intention of allowing me to slip into Ignacio's role."

Rever lifted the bar out of my hands and placed it on top of the bar catcher. "What do you mean, he wanted me to fail?"

"He said he planted ideas in your head, made things available." I lifted the bar again to do another set of reps. My entire body burned, but I couldn't stop. I'd go crazy. I'd been spinning my wheels to no end for days.

Shadows flickered through Rever's eyes. "You really think he could be working with Juan Alvarez?"

I lifted the weight bar eight more times, concentrating on the simultaneous burn and quiver of my pectoral muscles as I counted off the reps in my head.

Eight. Nine. Ten.

"No." I handed the bar to Rever. "I think he's playing Juan and Ignacio against each other."

"Why would he do that?"

I licked my lips. "Think about it. If both cartels are weakened by this turf war, it leaves the whole region open to being exploited by other cartels or new leadership."

Rever frowned. "How would that benefit Emanuel?"

I wiped my hand across my sweat stained forehead. "Emanuel wants to be the new leader to rise from the ashes, and consolidate the entire region under him. We all know he has people in the Alvarez Cartel feeding Emanuel information. Who's to say they're not working for both sides? I'm sure he has plenty of people loyal to him in the Vargas Cartel, but in order to unite everyone behind him, he needs to discredit both of Ignacio's potential successors. Your name is already shit, and that leaves me."

"And Juan's successor apparent is dead." Rever leaned his back against the wall behind him and tipped his head toward the ceiling.

I sat up and stretched my aching arm muscles over my head. "Yes, and Juan is in the hospital, and we killed almost all of his inner circle when we rescued Hattie."

"Now the attempt on Ignacio's life makes a lot of sense. I couldn't believe his guard screwed up and allowed him to get shot."

"Right, and who directs Ignacio's personal guard?" I asked, the pieces of the puzzle shifting into place in my mind.

Rever whistled under his breath. "Emanuel directs the *Fuerzas Especiales de Ignacio*," he said, referencing Ignacio's paramilitary unit.

"Dammit." I rubbed my temples. "If I suspected we were being manipulated, I would've let Enrique live. I played right into Emanuel's hands." Images of things Enrique did to Hattie flashed through my mind. "Then again, I probably still would've killed him for hurting Hattie."

"Fuck," Rever said, his voice rough.

"My thoughts exactly."

"So what are we going to do?" Rever asked.

"You're going to help me."

He nodded. "I'm in. That fucker has manipulated me for the last time."

I angled my chin to the side. "I have one condition."

"What's that?"

"Ignacio has to go too."

"You're planning to run the Vargas Cartel by yourself?"

"No," I said. "You're going to do it with me."

He pursed his lips. "I don't know. I think I'm

done with this."

"You owe me. I helped you with Anna."

Rever scoffed. "Yeah, well, that didn't turn out so great. She was jerking me around."

I shrugged. "A debt for a debt, remember?" I reminded him. He had promised me if I helped with Anna, he owed me a favor in the future.

"I remember." Rever scrubbed his hands over his face. "Why do you want my help running the cartel? What do I have to offer?"

"You know all the contacts. You know the history. I'd be running blind by myself."

"What's going to happen to Ignacio? Are you going to kill him?"

Standing up, I smiled. "No. I have other plans for him."

Rever's eyebrows lifted. "Should I ask?"

"No." I patted him on his shoulder. "But I think you'll like the outcome."

Chapter Twenty-One

Hattie

"We're wasting our time. There has to be another way," I complained as I sat on the sofa in Ryker's D.C. apartment to buckle my heels.

I hadn't done anything about my living situation. The majority of my stuff was still at Vera's apartment. She was my best friend, but after I saw the email she sent to Evan indicating she fed him information about me, I didn't fully trust her. Also, I couldn't imagine what she'd think if I showed up with Noah in tow.

He'd been my constant shadow for the last week, but tonight that was going to change. I'd promised to meet my parents at a restaurant for dinner tonight. Noah wanted to come with me, but I refused. Despite Noah's insistence that we could introduce him to my parents as a friend from college, I didn't think the lie would work. After hours of back and forth, we agreed he'd sit at the restaurant bar to keep an eye on me.

Noah glanced at his phone for a moment without

comment. "We're in luck. I have one more lead, and I don't have any doubts they'll print the story." He cocked a brow. "In fact, I know they will."

My heart skipped a beat. I'd love to wrap up this whole mess in the next couple of days. For the past week, I successfully avoided a confrontation with my parents and my professors while I focused all of my energy on exposing Senator Deveron. Unfortunately, my parents were getting increasingly suspicious.

First, I called them from Mexico pretending I'd taken a road trip to clear my head. Then, I didn't reach out to them for another week after being abducted by the Alvarez Cartel. My dad had filed a missing person's report when they couldn't reach me. Now that I'd been home a week, I couldn't avoid them any longer. I had to force myself to do normal things even though I felt as though my life had been turned upside down.

I grabbed my small rectangular black purse from the coffee table and opened the front door. "Are you going to tell me or were you planning to surprise me?"

He squeezed my upper arm. "I planned to tell you, but I don't think you'll like my idea."

I pressed the call button for the elevator. "What are you afraid of?"

He smirked. "That you'll refuse to cooperate."

"This doesn't sound promising." I groaned.

He lifted his eyebrows. "It's perfect, actually. We should've started there rather than with the more reputable places."

"Noah," I cautioned as we stepped into the

elevator. "You better tell me."

"Fine, but it's too late to cancel." He shrugged. "We're meeting a reporter from *Star Weekly* for coffee tomorrow morning."

I gaped at him. "You can't be serious."

He winked at me. "Dead serious."

I glared at him. "What the hell, Noah. I'm not entrusting this story to a grocery store tabloid. This isn't some guess about who's cheating or in rehab scandal. This is serious."

He laughed softly as he stepped out of the elevator and into the parking garage. "I realize that, but a tabloid will take chances a mainstream news agency won't. Think of the John Edwards love child scandal."

"Yes, that's my point exactly. That was a cheating scandal, involving an illegitimate love child. It belonged on the front page of a tabloid."

He opened the passenger door of Ryker's car and I slipped inside. It felt strange using all of Ryker's things while he was still in Mexico doing God only knows what. I broke down and called him yesterday to listen to his voicemail. Even though it was irrational, I had hoped he'd answer the phone.

He slipped into the driver's seat and drove out of the parking garage. "Look, I know it's not ideal, but at least the story will be out in the open. Once they let the cat out of the bag, some independent websites will cover it too, and the networks won't be able to ignore it. The story will have too much traction, especially with the mountain of evidence Ryker gave you."

"Yeah, maybe you're right," I said, staring at the

flickering lights of D.C. illuminating the dark sky. "I just wish we could've got it on the front pages of the major D.C. newspapers."

His jaw clenched as he tapped his fingers against the steering wheel. "Don't worry. It will get there. Senator Deveron won't be doing his backroom deals for much longer."

I stared at his profile, and I couldn't hold back any longer. "Why did you get involved with pay-for-hire mercenary work?"

Jarringly silent, Noah's eyes narrowed and his eyebrows slanted low over his light brown eyes. He seemed to be trying to figure out how to answer my question, but then it hit me. He had no intention of telling me anything about him. I'd spent the last week living in his pocket, and he knew everything about me, and I didn't know more than a few inconsequential facts about him. I was so tired of all the secrets, lies, and half-truths.

"It pays well, and it's never boring. Not many people can say the same thing about their jobs," he finally answered.

"Do you have a family?" I asked.

He white-knuckled the steering wheel. "Nope."

I chewed my lip, taking in the sharp angles of his profile and his heavily lashed eyes. "Everybody has a family."

"I don't," he snapped, his eyes darkening.

I rolled my eyes. "So you were born in a test tube and raised in an orphanage?"

"Drop it, Hattie," he growled, his lips thinning. "You know all you need to know about me. We aren't friends. I'm doing a job."

My shoulders tensed, and I folded my arms across my body. "Fine. I don't mind being strangers. We'll only communicate when absolutely necessary. How does that sound?"

His frown deepened. "Perfect," he answered without glancing at me.

"Great." I leaned forward and turned up the volume of the radio.

I stared out the window. Trees lined the street. The yellow glow of lights from the inside the buildings dotted the sidewalk. Couples strolled hand and hand. Laughter floated through the air from the restaurants. Everything looked normal. Simple even. Jealousy ate at my insides. I missed my uncomplicated life where I didn't have to second-guess everyone and everything.

Noah turned down the volume and pulled the car over to the side of the road. "My job requires anonymity and you're safer the less you know about me." He threaded his fingers through his hair. "I shouldn't have taken this job. I just..." His voice faded, and I didn't think he'd say anything else. "I don't know. I wanted to help you. Let's leave it at that."

"Okay," I rasped, forcing a weak smile. From the look on his face, it resembled more of a grimace than a smile.

He gestured to the valet stand on the sidewalk, looking pained. "We're here. You go ahead. I'll see you inside in a few minutes. I have to make a call."

I cracked open the door and slipped one leg out the door. "Wait." I glanced over my shoulder. "Are you calling Ryker?"

His shoulders hiked up. "Yes."

I pulled my leg back into the car and closed the door. "I want to talk to him."

"No." He leaned over me and opened the door again. "Get out."

"He'll want to talk to me too."

"You can call him after the meeting tomorrow if he gives me the green light." He shoved me lightly on my shoulder. "Now leave. You're already five minutes late. Your parents are going to start calling."

I frowned. "I just want to say hi. That's it."

He pointed at the door. "Tomorrow. That's as good as I can do."

I rolled my eyes and then my phone rang, as if my parents knew I wanted to back out of dinner. I glanced at the screen. It was my mom. "Fine. See you in a few minutes."

"Text me if you need anything," he said as I climbed out of the car. "And don't leave without me."

"Yeah. Yeah," I mumbled, nodding my head. "I won't go anywhere without you. I know the drill."

Chapter Twenty~Two

Hattie

"Hi," I said as I bent to kiss my mom's stiff cheek.

My mom smiled tepidly. "It's good to see you, Hattie. We were beginning to think you weren't going to show."

"Oh. I'm sorry." I forced a smile on my face as I unfolded my napkin and arranged it on my lap. "I'm only a couple of minutes late. It took longer than I thought to get here."

"Don't pick on her, Elaine," my dad griped, his eyes narrowing fractionally. "We weren't waiting more than a couple of minutes. You're going to scare her away again."

I glanced back and forth between my mom and dad. Normally, they presented a unified front, but something told me that wasn't the case right now. The tension between them was palpable.

My mom cocked her perfectly coiffed blonde head to the side. "She should show us the respect we deserve. She disappeared on a road trip without a word. Then, she didn't bother to come see us for a week after she returned home."

I tugged on the edge of the sleeve of my silk blouse. It barely covered my burn marks, but wearing a long-sleeved shirt in the middle of the summer would look suspicious. "You're right. I should've stopped by the house, but I've been busy."

My mom's sculpted eyebrow lifted. "Doing what? You haven't touched base with your professors in three weeks. You haven't called Evan. I don't even know where you're living. I called Vera, and she hasn't seen you either."

The metal legs scraped across the hardwood floor as I slid my chair away from the table and tossed my napkin on the table. Anger lit my veins on fire. How dare she pry into my life? How dare she bring up Evan? "I don't know why I bothered to come here tonight. For some reason, I keep giving you the benefit of the doubt." I shook my head. "I should know better by now. I need to stop wasting my time."

My mom stared down her nose at me. "I could say the same thing verbatim to you."

I leaned back in my chair. "What the hell is that supposed to mean?"

"It's time you stopped this nonsense and pulled your life together. You're all over the place. You got engaged. You dropped out of your master's program. You terminated your internship. You ended your engagement. You moved in with Vera. You reenrolled in the master's program. You disappeared on a road trip." She punctuated each point with a flick of her blood-red fingernails.

"Nonsense?" I echoed. "In case you've forgotten, I experienced some traumatic things lately, not that you care. All you care about is preventing the chaos from spilling over into your perfect little world."

My dad slammed his hand on the table. The water glasses shook, and the silverware rattled. "Dammit, Elaine, this is not the time to scrutinize every decision she's made in the past few months. We agreed we'd have dinner without diving into anything confrontational. Give her time to come to terms with everything and put her life back together. You need to know when to stop pushing so hard. She'll come around."

"She's had plenty of time," my mom mumbled under her breath.

Even though my gut churned with resentment, I schooled my face into a blank mask, trying to hide all my emotions. My mom preyed on insecurities. "I don't need time. My life is just fine." I lifted the glass of ice water to my lips.

My mom gasped. "Are you engaged?"

My stomach dropped. I'd forgotten to take off Ryker's engagement ring before dinner. I'd been running late after another unsuccessful meeting with a small D.C. magazine. I stared at my parents for a long moment, then cleared my throat. "Kind of," I answered, inwardly cursing the tremble in my voice. Ryker and I weren't technically engaged, but I couldn't explain the details of our promise to each other.

My dad pursed his lips. "Kind of? What's that supposed to mean?"

"We're still working things out. You know, school, living arrangements and other stuff," I murmured, hating, and not for the first time, that things between us weren't simple.

My mom pressed her hand to her chest, her eyes wide with panic. "You haven't talked to Evan for weeks. What's going on?"

Twirling a strand of hair around my finger, I squinted across the room, trying to find anything to look at other than either of my parents' faces. "This has nothing to do with Evan. I met someone else."

"When?"

I moved my hands into my lap and twisted the ends of my napkin. "I've known him for a few months," I answered vaguely. "I know it seems sudden, but I love him."

My mom's brows knitted together, disgust contorting her lips into a scowl. "You met him when you were engaged to Evan?"

I sat awkwardly, heat rushing to my face under the intense stare of both my parents. Part of me longed to burst out laughing and claim the whole thing was a joke gone awry, but I knew I couldn't. This was just the beginning. I needed to break my parents' hold on me once and for all and make my own decisions. As a child, my mom had used every psychological trick in her arsenal to mold me into the person she wanted me to be. The moment I left for college, I started pushing back, but I had never managed to eliminate her control entirely.

I squeezed my hands into tight balls and drew in a deep breath through my nose, summoning my willpower. "No, before that."

"I don't understand," my mom said, her voice hushed as though she suddenly realized she didn't want anyone to overhear our conversation.

"What's to understand? I met someone I want to spend my life with," I snarled, unable to control my growing temper. "You don't need to understand. You need to support me."

"But you haven't even introduced him to us, and I'm not sure you've recovered." She leaned closer to me and her heavy floral scent curled around my nose. "Don't you think this is too sudden? I mean, what will we tell everyone? A month or so ago you were engaged to Evan, and now you're engaged to someone new. That doesn't look good."

I sat taller in my chair and squared my shoulders, refusing to bow under the weight of my mom's glare. She'd never change. She thought she knew how I should live my life. She was wrong. If she thought I'd bend to her will right now, she didn't know me at all. I'd been subjected to far worse at the hands of the Alvarez Cartel. She could dump a mountain of guilt on me, glare at me until her eye sockets froze, but I wouldn't leave Ryker or change my course. I was a fighter, and I planned to fight for Ryker and our child every step of the way.

"Evan was a mistake. He asked me to marry him when I wasn't thinking clearly. If I hadn't been emotionally vulnerable and exhausted, I never would've agreed. I hate him. I hate his family." I pinned her with my eyes, daring her to challenge me.

My mom sucked in a breath, and her face flushed red. The air buzzed with years of mutual anger and resentment.

My dad waved his hand in front of his face. The three of us sat in silence. His expression held no sign of judgment. I listened to the low hum of restaurant, picking up fragments of conversation from nearby tables.

"Hattie, are you happy? Does he make your happy?" he asked as he rubbed the back of his neck.

I nodded. "Yes. Very much."

My dad leaned forward and tapped his fingers on the white tablecloth. Every thud sent my heart higher and higher until every frazzled beat vibrated at the back of my throat, suffocating me.

He blew out a breath. "That's all that matters. Why didn't you bring him tonight? Do we know him?"

"His name is Ryker and he's out of town right now."

"Are you living at his house?"

"Yes." I shrugged. "For now. He's out of town for a couple more weeks, and I still don't have anywhere to live. It made sense."

"Right." My mom nodded. "What does he do?"

Here came the unanswerable questions. My body sagged like someone had placed a hundred-pound weight on my head. "Oh, I don't know. It's hard to explain."

My dad's eyes narrowed. "Is he employed or does he plan to live off you and your family?"

My anger flared, but I bit the inside of my cheek, pushing back the emotion. I didn't want to pick another fight tonight. "He does consulting. He doesn't need your connections or your money." I lifted my chin. "Neither do I."

"Those are big words for a girl who doesn't have a job and hasn't finished her master's," my mother said.

The words hit me like a punch to the gut, which was fitting. My mom excelled at low blows. "I'm fine. You and dad don't need to worry about me. My life is back on track again. I know what I want."

I looked over my shoulder, and my gaze collided with Noah's. He didn't even pretend to blend with the other patrons at the bar. All of his attention was focused on my family and me. I flashed him a small, quick smile and turned back to my parents.

Desperately seeking a diversion, I lifted my menu, concealing my face. "What's good here? I haven't had a thing to eat since breakfast. I'm starving."

My dad smiled. "You do seem happier than you've been in a long time."

"I am."

My dad nodded. "I can't wait to meet the guy who changed your life."

"Soon," I promised, even though I didn't know if it would ever happen.

So many things had to come to pass before we could be together. Did it make me a terrible person that I didn't care who we had to hurt to get what we wanted?

My mind whirled with a million and one questions. I shook my head and pushed it all away. I was getting too far ahead of myself. I needed to move forward one step at a time, and step one was making it through dinner with my parents.

Chapter Twenty~Three

Ryker

Yellow, pink, and orange streaks tinted the late afternoon sky. Rever's bright yellow convertible Porsche darted in and out of traffic along the coastal highway, drawing more than a few stares. Wind tunneled through my hair and the smell of exhaust burned my nostrils.

"Couldn't we have driven something less conspicuous?" I yelled.

"Nah," Rever responded without looking at me. "Everyone knows this is my car."

"Exactly my point," I grumbled.

Rever chuckled. "Everyone will stay clear of us when we're driving home. It's perfect."

"Right, but everyone will know our whereabouts tonight. That's what I'm worried about."

"They'll know we're in Playa del Carmen for dinner, but they won't know anything more than that. It's the perfect cover."

"I hope you're right," I mumbled more to myself than him.

A wide grin stretched across his face as we darted across traffic, earning more than a few honks and angry hand gestures. "Trust me. You'll see. Besides, if our suspicions are correct, it won't matter in a couple days."

"I have a feeling you've done something like this before."

"Not exactly." His tires squealed as he slammed on his brakes and reversed into a tight spot next to the high-curbed sidewalk.

We both got out of the car, and Rever pointed to a restaurant with an open-air patio. "I hope you like Italian food."

I shrugged as Rever greeted the hostess. "Does it matter?"

"Not really. We'll sit down for five minutes, then make our way out the back door of the restaurant. Nobody will suspect a thing and if they do...fuck 'em."

"If you say so," I said as we strolled through the restaurant to a table near the kitchen.

Heads turned in waves, watching every move we made. Murmurs and hushed whispers followed us like ghosts. I kept my chin up, and my eyes focused on the back wall. I couldn't imagine a day when I would get used to the attention of being affiliated with the Vargas Cartel. For the most part, Ignacio confined me to the compound as a child, but on occasion he took me out and flaunted our connection. I still hated the way stares filled with fear followed me everywhere.

I settled into the chair across from Rever, stretching my legs out to the side with my back pressed into the wall. Rever was confident our high profile would shield us. I didn't agree. The war with the Alvarez Cartel had eroded some of Ignacio's power. Killing Enrique Alvarez had halted the power shift, but it left us susceptible to challenge.

Rever scanned the menu, commenting about the food he liked. I didn't respond. Instead, I watched the restaurant staff and fellow patrons studiously avoid eye contact. Even the tourists avoided looking our way despite the fact that they were generally oblivious to the ugly side of Mexico. They viewed Mexico as a relatively inexpensive vacation with free flowing alcohol and long sandy beaches. As an unspoken rule, the cartels didn't allow the violence to spill into tourist areas, but it happened on occasion.

"Why is everyone starting at us?"

Rever looked up from the laminated menu and tapped the corner of the wooden table. "Get used to it."

"How do they know who we are?"

"The staff probably knows or suspects something and the rest of them are sensing the tension."

"Maybe," I said noncommittally.

Rever stood. "All right. Let's get out of here."

"How far is the walk?" I asked, following him.

"A couple of blocks. Maybe less, but either way he won't have any idea we're coming."

I fingered the top of my gun under my linen blazer. Sweat trickled down the middle of my back, and I wanted to strip off the jacket and dump it in the trash, but Mexican gun laws were really strict. I didn't want to be caught on the wrong side of the law right now. Ignacio had plenty of governmental officials on his payroll, and he could make the charge disappear with one phone call, but I couldn't stomach being indebted to him for anything else.

Five minutes later Rever paused in front of the blue door of Emanuel's house. He slipped his gun from the holster behind his back. "I'm going in first."

I nodded. "I've got your back."

Rever glanced over his shoulder, a wide smile on his face. "You better, asshole. This was all your idea. If it fails, I'm blaming you."

He didn't wait for my response. He shot the deadbolt on the door. The wood splintered, and I shaded my face, protecting my eyes from the flying debris. With his gun in front of his body, he kicked the door open. Following his lead, I slid my gun out of the holster.

Emanuel stepped out of the shadows, his gun drawn. "What the hell are you two doing here?"

"Put your gun down before I put a bullet between your eyes," Rever said, his voice cold as ice.

The veins on the side of Emanuel's neck pulsed with anger. "Ignacio is going to kill both of you."

"We'll take our chances with Ignacio." I pulled the trigger of my gun and successfully shot him in the foot, immobilizing him.

The gun slipped from his hand, and he stumbled forward onto one knee. "What the fuck is wrong with you?"

"You know," I started, "after I talked to you last week, I had an epiphany." I tapped my gun against my thigh.

"You're crazy," he growled through clenched teeth.

"All this time, you were pretending to be Ignacio's faithful servant without any ambition for more," I continued, ignoring his words. "Then, I realized you not only wanted more, but you were also actively manipulating Ignacio and Juan to consolidate the resources of the two most powerful cartels in this region behind you. Only Ignacio and Juan were too stupid to see you for what you are."

"You'll never prove anything," he taunted, reaching for his gun on the floor in front of him.

Pop!

I shot his hand.

"You piece of shit. You're going to kill me."

"He's right," Rever said, his voice eerily flat. "You shouldn't toy with him before we get him to the torture room. If he loses too much blood, we'll have to let him recover before the fun starts, and I'm in the mood to see lots of blood. I have so many plans for him."

I shrugged. "I don't know. I'm an immediate gratification type of guy. Maybe we could do it here."

"Nah. We have better tools at the compound. We should wait."

Emanuel grabbed a knife from the inside of his pant leg. He lurched forward and it flew through the air in slow motion heading for Rever.

"Rever, watch out," I screamed, but it was too late.

The knife plunged into Rever's shoulder. He

staggered backward, falling to his knees. His eyes widened, and his lips parted. I charged forward, tackling Emanuel. His head cracked against the tile floor. My legs straddling his waist, I wrapped my hands around his neck. Emanuel clawed at my arm, but I didn't feel anything. I wanted to strangle the life from his body second by second. His lips turned blue. His eyes bulged. His legs twitched. A haze of red filled my vision as I summoned the specter of death with my bare hands.

"That's enough," Rever grunted. He pulled the knife from his shoulder and tossed it on the floor. Blood oozed out of his wound, staining his white shirt.

"No." I tightened my hands around his neck. "He helped Juan Alvarez abduct Hattie. She could've been killed."

Rever slid a pair of handcuffs across the floor. "Yeah, well, we need to get a confession before you kill him. Otherwise, we'll never get Ignacio to do what we want him to do."

My body sagged, and my grip on his neck loosened. "Fuck," I yelled, slamming my fist into the wall behind me. White dust coated my knuckles.

"Don't worry. You'll get the chance to do whatever you want with him," Rever said, cupping his shoulder. Blood seeped through his fingers.

I spat on Emanuel's face and flipped him onto his back. I snapped one ring of the cuffs around his wrist and the other around the iron stair railing.

"Take my car keys," Rever said, dangling them from his fingers.

I snatched them out of his hand and started

moving toward the front door.

"Text me when you're out front and get the duct tape out of the glove box."

"I'm on it. See you in a few minutes."

"Hurry the fuck up. I don't want to get in a gun fight while you're gone." His hardened gaze drifted across the room. "I have to find some bleach to clean this mess up. I don't want it to look like we murdered someone in here." He chuckled at his own joke. "That'll come later. Much later."

Chapter Twenty-Four

Hattie

Sunlight streamed through the edges of the dark brown wooden blinds. I stretched my arms over my head, rolled onto my side and inhaled. Even though weeks had passed since Ryker had slept in this bed, I pretended I could smell his scent. Honestly, it smelled more like laundry detergent than anything else.

"You're awake. I was afraid you planned to sleep until lunchtime," Noah said, tapping a magazine against his thigh. A slim bar of light slashed across the sharp angles of his face, making the lower half light and the upper half dark.

"I was tired. I didn't go to bed until late." I scooted up to the headboard. "Speaking of which, have you heard from Ryker?"

"No." He glanced to the side, his eyes distant. "Nothing."

I eyed him somberly, wishing I could ignore the persistent stabbing in my chest. "But you've heard something, right?"

He scrubbed his hand down the side of his face. "Just that there are some internal power struggles going on inside the Vargas Cartel."

I buried my hands in the sheets. "You're scaring me. What does that mean?"

Leaning forward, he rested his elbows on his knees. The rolled up magazine dangled from one hand. "I don't have all the details."

"What details do you have?"

"Emanuel, Ignacio's right-hand man, disappeared a couple of days ago. His apartment was covered in blood. Nobody knows if he's alive. Rumors place Rever and Ryker in the area around the time he went missing, but that doesn't mean a whole helluva a lot."

I cringed. "Do you think they killed him?"

"If they haven't killed him, they will soon."

My mouth dropped open, and my gut heaved. "Seriously? Why would they do that?"

"I don't know for sure." He exhaled, unrolled the magazine and held up the cover for me to see it. "On a different note, we did it."

I scanned the glossy cover. Senator Deveron had his head bowed, and dark sunglasses covered his eyes. A blurb on the left-hand column in bright yellow print said, *Senator Deveron funded by Mexican drug cartels*.

I jumped out of bed and snatched the magazine out of his hand. "I didn't believe they'd actually do it."

Noah stood. "Go to page ten."

I flipped open the magazine and scanned the story. "This is so good. They didn't hold back at all."

"Nope."

I closed the magazine. "So what happens now?"

"We sit back and watch the show. The mainstream media has picked up the story. It's only a matter of time before he's forced to resign."

A warm glow trickled through my veins. For the first time in two weeks, I could finally breathe. "Do you think he'll go to jail?"

"He should." Noah shrugged, a mischievous smile spreading across his face. "I think that's up to the Department of Justice, but I think you have some strings you can pull there," he said, referencing my dad.

"You're right." I tossed the magazine on top of the bed and wrapped my arms around his waist. "Thanks so much for your help. I know Ryker's paying you, but you didn't have to do it. You probably have better things to do than play babysitter and accompany me to meetings."

He leaned back and my hands slid from his body. "I would've done it for free." He brushed his knuckles along my jaw, and my heart tripped in my chest. "You needed help and I wanted to be the one to help you. You didn't deserve what happened to you."

Unease trickled down my spine. I laughed nervously and backpedaled a few steps, my eyes trained on the grains of hardwood beneath my bare feet.

"It all worked out. It led me to Ryker so I can't be mad about that. He makes me happy."

He took one step closer to me, his golden eyes

focused on me with enough heat to unnerve me. The air around us pressed against my chest, suffocating me. "Does he really make you happy or is that just what you want to believe?"

I shook my head slowly from side to side, never taking my eyes off him. "Noah, what's going on? What are you doing?"

He grabbed my hand. "Why are you with Ryker?"

My throat thickened. "Because I love him," I choked out.

His lips pursed into a tight line. "Do you really? Or are you just holding onto him because you don't feel like you have anyone else who cares about you? Or because of the baby?"

Tension curled my muscles into tight balls, and my pulse galloped inside my chest. "I don't need to explain anything to you." I yanked my hand away from him.

"You do understand that Ryker and Rever are trying to wrestle control of the Vargas Cartel from Ignacio."

"Why would they do that? Neither of them wants anything to do with it."

"They didn't want anything to do with the cartel when it meant being controlled by Ignacio. If they could call the shots, they might feel differently. That's what is going on right now, or at least that's what my sources suspect."

Stunned, hurt, and angry didn't begin to express how I felt at that moment. My stomach swirled uncomfortably, and my knees wilted. I stumbled backward and sat on the bed. "Why didn't you tell me that earlier?"

"I didn't want to spell it out. I wanted you to read between the lines."

I pressed my palms into my eyes, willing the tears to disappear. I needed to be strong. I promised Ryker I'd be strong. He promised we'd end up together, and I still wanted a life with him even if it meant I'd be the wife of a notorious drug lord. I nearly laughed at the ridiculousness of my reality.

"Do you realize what you'll be giving up to be with him?"

My hands dropped from my face. "I think I have an idea?" The words came out as a question.

"You'd be ostracized by your family. You won't be able to come back to the States. Ryker would keep you tucked away in a glass cage for the rest of your—"

"No, he wouldn't," I said, interrupting him.

"He wouldn't have any choice. If he didn't, his rivals would use you to get to him."

Even though I wanted to sink to my knees, I pretended to be unfazed. I stood, ignoring the sinking feeling in my gut. "I trust Ryker. He would never do anything like that." I flipped my hair over my shoulder. "I need to get dressed. Please leave."

His heated stare settled on me, and it felt like I was standing in front of the pearly gates on judgment day. My gaze dipped to my feet, and I studied the circular grains on the hardwood floor. I had to look away. Otherwise, I think I would've shattered into a million unrecognizable pieces.

"Think about it, Hattie. You're not meant for that kind of life. You need to find someone who's willing to choose you over everything."

Spots dotted my vision and anger gnawed at my heart. I wouldn't leave him, not even if it meant a lifetime as part of the Vargas Cartel. I wasn't stupid. I understood what kind of things he'd have to do if he succeeded. He'd kill and torture people, but none of that would stop me from loving him. When I looked at Ryker, I'd always see who he was deep down in his heart.

"Ryker is that person," I hissed. "Stop this." I sliced my hand through the air. "Whatever it is. I know what I'm doing. I understand the risks. I don't expect everything to be perfect, but I do expect you to keep your opinion to yourself unless I ask you for it."

He raked his hands through his hair. Disapproval etched deep grooves into his forehead. "You're right. I should keep my opinions to myself. I shouldn't ask all the questions that come to mind." He smiled, but he looked pained. "But if you need help getting away or you realize you're in over your head, I'll help you. All you have to do is call. You know that, right?"

I nodded, my insides coiling from the sincerity in his eyes. "Thanks, Noah. I appreciate the offer. I really do, but I knew when I chose Ryker that everything wouldn't be sunshine and rainbows. I'm not going to back out now." He opened his mouth to respond, and I shook my head. "I don't want to back out."

He sighed and walked toward the door. "All right, Hattie. I won't say anything else. Just know the option is always there whether it's two months or two years from now."

My heart constricted at his protective words. "Why do you want to help me?"

He lifted one shoulder, a faint smile on his lips. "You remind me of someone I used to know."

"Do you want to elaborate?"

"Maybe some other time."

I nodded. "How long are you sticking around here?"

"Actually, I'm leaving this afternoon. I have a new assignment overseas."

His gaze lingered on me for a moment and then he closed the door softly. I sat on the edge of the bed and bowed my head. I hoped Ryker made good on his promises because I had successfully alienated everyone who had ever cared about me.

Chapter Twenty~Five

Ryker

Rever finished tying Emanuel's legs and arms to the chair and then he rolled his sleeves to his elbows.

"Point the camera over here," Rever said as he pulled the pillowcase off Emanuel's head. "And make sure you get his entire body on the screen."

After we arrived at the compound yesterday, we did a half-assed job at patching up Emanuel's wounds, and left him shackled to the wall in the same shack where I'd housed Hattie months ago. Today, we needed to do everything possible to get Emanuel to confess on tape. We wouldn't kill him, though. We'd save that decision for Ignacio.

I angled the tripod to capture Emanuel's entire body on the video and peeked through the lens. "I think I've got it."

"Good." Rever twirled his knife through his fingers like a baton. "I think I'll spare you the explanation of what's going to happen now," Rever said as he circled Emanuel's chair. "We all have intimate knowledge of how these types of interrogations work."

Emanuel spit on the floor in front of him, narrowly missing Rever's shoes. *"Chinga tu madre."*

Rever chuckled. "You're lucky I'm not very fond of my mother either or I might be tempted to cut off your cock for talking about her like that."

Emanuel's eyes narrowed into slits. "You can do whatever you want. I won't tell you anything."

"How do you think we should start?" Rever ran the knife along the tips of his fingers, testing the sharpness of the blade. "I've always been a fan of starting small." He shrugged. "You know...fingers, toes, ears. I don't want him to lose consciousness too soon."

I pointed to the small water buckets lining the wall. "I've always wanted to see waterboarding in action. I'd like to know what all the fuss is about."

Rever sucked his lips into his mouth as he angled his head to the side. "Good idea. I think you're right. It's an efficient method of breaking someone without causing a mortal injury. Most of the time, anyway."

I lifted the bucket of water. "Do you want to tip the chair back or pour the water?"

"I'll hold the chair," Rever said. He tipped chair backward, lifting the front legs off the ground so that Emanuel's lungs were higher than his mouth to avoid total suffocation.

I pulled a thin white rag from my back pocket and draped it over his eyes. I lifted the bucket and poured water on the rag. With one hand, Rever slowly lowered the saturated rag until it covered

Emanuel's mouth and his upturned nose. He put his hand over the wet rag, suffocating him for thirty seconds to increase the carbon dioxide level in Emanuel's bloodstream. When Rever lifted his hand, I dumped water over the rag for sixty seconds. Then, Rever ripped the rag off his face. Emanuel gagged, sucking in three giant mouthfuls of air. He slapped the rag over his face and started the process again. We repeated the entire thing a half dozen times until Emanuel's lips were blue, and his entire body trembled.

Rever slammed all four legs of Emanuel's chair on the ground. "Are you working with Juan Alvarez?"

"Fuck you," Emanuel said, his voice hoarse.

Rever crouched on the floor and plunged his knife under Emanuel big toenail. He twisted the knife in a seesawing motion until the toenail peeled off Emanuel's foot.

A scream echoed through the room, and Emanuel jerked against his restraints. Blood pooled on the cement floor beneath his foot.

"Do you want to answer me now?" Rever barked.

Emanuel glared, his entire body vibrating with anger and hatred. He clenched his jaw, his eyes blinking rapidly. "Go to hell! You can do this for days, and I won't tell you a damn thing."

"My pleasure. I was just getting started," Rever said, thrusting his knife under the next toenail. Bile rolled in my stomach as another bloody nail skittered across the floor, brushing the tip of my shoe. Emanuel sagged in his chair.

It didn't look like Rever minded the violence. In

fact, he seemed to be in his element. Inhaling through my mouth, I suppressed the urge to vomit on the floor. Emanuel had to believe Rever and I were united in everything in order for this to work. Likewise, I'd be dumb to expose any weaknesses to Rever. We were brothers, but loyalty only stretched so far in our world. Loyalties shifted like the wind. Money and power spoke louder than blood ties.

"Do you have anything to tell me now?" Rever yelled.

"I paid the Alvarez whore to ride your dick. Did she tell you that? She fucks any guy who shows interest, but I had to pay her to fuck you," Emanuel sneered. "How does that make you feel?"

Rever lurched forward, slamming his fist into Emanuel's jaw. His head pitched backward, and blood mixed with spittle showered the front of Rever's shirt.

"You're pathetic," Emanuel growled. Blood dripped down his chin from the corner of his mouth. "No wonder Ignacio begged Ryker to help him. You're so easy to manipulate."

Rever jabbed the tip of his knife into Emanuel's neck. "I should kill you right now."

Emanuel lifted his chin, his dark eyes sizzling with undisguised anger. "Do it. I dare you."

I clamped my hand around Rever's wrist. His muscles coiled under my fingers and his eyes glittered. The coppery scent of blood settled in the air like a heavy mist, clogging my throat and clinging to my skin.

"Don't let him get to you," I hissed. "He's trying to rattle you. He wants you to kill him quickly because he knows it's better than the alternative."

Rever closed his eyes and inhaled, his nostrils flaring. His right eyelid twitched and the muscles in his forearms corded. The seconds ticked like hours. Then, he nodded and yanked his wrist from my hold.

"What do you think, Ryker? Another toenail or should I start cutting off fingers?" He waved his knife back and forth between Emanuel's hands and feet like a music conductor.

I shifted my weight as I pretended to consider the question. "Finish the toenails on that foot, then move to his hand on the opposite of his body," I said.

Rever laughed. "I like how you think, Ryker."

I'd roughed people up in the past, but I'd never crossed the line into the world of torture. I should've been revolted and horrified, but the longer I watched Rever, the more immune I became to Emanuel's pain. With every toenail that flicked across the room, the pain lining Emanuel's face bothered me less and less. Black and white no longer existed. Everything was colored in shades of gray.

Maybe I'd regret this later, but for now, I felt vindicated and refreshed. Emanuel had manipulated Ignacio, Rever, Juan Alvarez, and me to some extent. This was the price of his arrogance. My stomach clenched at the thought. How much longer until I embraced Ignacio's philosophy of killing and torturing traitors to the fullest extent? How much longer until I was a mirror image of my father?

"Okay. Okay. I'll tell you whatever you want to know," Emanuel yelled, interrupting my train of thought. His entire body shivered and red lines mapped the whites of his eyes. "Just stop. I can't take any more."

Rever had removed five toenails and one fingernail. Blood seeped out of Emanuel's foot in a slow trickle. Cuts and bruises covered his face. He'd lost consciousness once, but I had dumped a bucket of ice water on his head and Rever kept going.

"Start talking," I said as I paced back on forth, my hands shoved deep into my pockets.

"Can you take off the handcuffs?"

"No," I said.

Emanuel closed his eyes and for a minute I thought I'd need to pour ice water on him again. "It started two years ago. I had a gambling debt, and I needed extra money."

"Why didn't you ask Ignacio for the money?"

"I did. I didn't tell him why I wanted it. I said I wanted to invest in a condominium project south of Playa del Carmen. Ignacio refused to advance me the money. Juan Alvarez was happy to. I tried to pay him back, but he didn't want money. He wanted information."

"What kind of information?" Rever asked, scratching a few specks of dry blood off his neck.

Emanuel's gaze drifted to the ceiling, and he cleared his throat. "Different stuff. Some of it was inconsequential. Some of it wasn't."

I tunneled my hands into my hair. "We need to know the details. Dates. Times. The information exchanged."

Emanuel dropped his chin to his chest. "I don't

remember everything."

Rever slapped him across his cheek. "Stop procrastinating. Tell us what you remember."

"It started small. He wanted names of government officials who were open to bribes. Next, he wanted names of people within the Vargas Cartel who had issues with Ignacio."

"Wait." I sliced my hand through the air. "You were working with Dario, weren't you?" I asked, referring to the man I killed when Hattie escaped from the Vargas Compound. Dario and three other men had surrounded us in the jungle. We killed them all and Ignacio killed Dario's son as payback. Then, the war between the Alvarez and Vargas Cartels exploded, making news throughout Mexico and the US.

Emanuel licked his lower lip. "I facilitated the introduction. I wasn't working with him."

I pinched the bridge of my nose. "What else?"

He shrugged. "I persuaded Juan Alvarez to use Anna to manipulate Rever."

"How the fuck would that help you?" Rever yelled.

"She got you out of the picture."

"So?" Rever spat.

"When Ignacio's successor abandoned him, it made him look incompetent. People were nervous about the future, which made it easy to find someone to kill Ignacio, but he survived."

"You were behind Ignacio's assassination attempt," I confirmed.

"Yes, but the whole thing backfired. Juan blackmailed me for the name of Hattie's hotel. I thought Ryker would rescue Hattie and flee the country, but Ignacio used the situation to solidify his hold on Ryker and find a new successor."

"So you were working for Juan Alvarez all along?" Rever asked.

"No," Emanuel scoffed, shaking his head. "I was working for myself. I wanted to weaken both cartels so I could unite everyone under me."

"Why?" I asked.

"I paid my dues, but no matter how hard I worked Ignacio refused to change his mind. He didn't think I was worthy of taking the reins."

"You're not. You're a piece of shit," Rever roared as his fist smashed into Emanuel's face. His eyes rolled up in their sockets, and his head lolled to the side like a rag doll.

"What the hell?" I said, eyeing Rever.

"I couldn't stand listening to him for one more second."

"Didn't you want to know anything else?"

"No." He dipped his bloodied hands into a bucket of water. "We have everything we need. Get the camera. Let's find Ignacio. He can finish this. I can't stand to breathe the same air as him for one more second. I can't believe I ever trusted him."

A choked laugh tumbled from my mouth as I turned off the camera.

"What's so funny?" Rever asked.

"All of Ignacio's paranoia was pointless."

"What do you mean?"

"He focused on everyone else while Emanuel snaked his way into every part of the cartel and betrayed him over and over."

Rever laughed then too. "You're right, and Ignacio accused *me* of being a dumbass."

Chapter Twenty~Six

Hattie

"I'm surprised to see you here," I said as I cracked open the door to Ryker's apartment.

"You haven't answered my calls for two days," my dad said as he shifted on his feet. Dark purplish circles stained the skin under his eyes. He wore a wrinkled t-shirt and jeans instead of a dark suit. I couldn't remember the last time I'd seen him dress casually.

I glanced to the side, unable to maintain eye contact with him. It hurt too much. I had begged him to come over and discuss everything that happened with Senator Deveron after the story broke, but he rejected my invitation.

"I don't have anything to say to you or Mom." My voice trembled, and I choked back a sob.

His nostrils flared. "Can I come in?"

"Is Mom with you?"

"No," he answered, shaking his head. "I thought it'd be better if I came alone."

"You can come in." I opened the door wider and

closed it behind him. "Do you want anything to drink?" I asked as we moved through the apartment.

"No. I'm good." He settled onto the sofa in the living room.

I sat on the chair across from him. "What did you want to talk about?"

He ran his hands along the tops of his thighs. "Mostly, I want to apologize for not coming over after the story about Senator Deveron came to light."

I raised one eyebrow, already feeling drained by this conversation. "An apology. That's it?"

He pursed his lips. "This is hard for me, Hattie."

I leaned back in the chair and folded my arms across my chest. "Yeah, I can imagine how hard it is for parents to support their child and believe them. I'd always thought it was something that came naturally, but apparently not," I said, my voice laced with sarcasm.

My dad held up his hand. "To be fair, your mom didn't tell me anything about your suspicions of Senator Deveron."

"Really? I find that hard to believe." I'd told my mom Senator Deveron had orchestrated my abduction by the Vargas Cartel, but she believed Evan over me and dismissed my accusation as a sign of Stockholm syndrome.

He exhaled and squared his shoulders, staring out the window. "She didn't say anything right away. She mentioned it during your road trip when we couldn't get in touch with you for a few weeks."

"And you didn't bother to talk to me about it." The words tasted like ash on my tongue.

"For the most part."

My brows scrunched together. "What's that supposed to mean?"

"I did some digging into a possible connection between the Vargas Cartel and Senator Deveron."

I unfolded my arms, and tapped my fingers on the armrests. "Did you find anything?"

"Nothing concrete. I found curious coincidences, though."

"But you didn't do anything about it."

"I didn't have the chance to decide one way or another before the whole story landed on the front page of a trashy grocery store tabloid. Did you have anything to do with that? The identity of the source is protected."

My gaze darted to the side as I contemplated how much to tell him. "Yes." I sighed. "I gave them the story along with the backup documentation."

"Where'd you get the information?"

I rubbed my hands over my lips. "I lied. I didn't go on a road trip a few weeks ago. I went to Mexico. I ended up at the Vargas compound. I got the information when I was there, and a friend helped me shop the information around. That trashy *grocery store tabloid* was the only place with enough guts to print the story."

He opened, then closed his mouth in quick succession. "Jesus, Hattie. I don't know what to say."

I rolled back my shoulders. "I did what I had to do. I couldn't let him get away with what he did to me."

"Do you have any idea what the Vargas Cartel

will do to you if they realize you are the source behind that article?" He tugged on the ends of his hair. "They will come after you and they will kill you."

I smiled condescendingly. "You're wrong. You don't know what you're talking about. They aren't going to do anything to me."

He jumped to his feet, his eyes wild. "Maybe you think they won't hurt you because they let you walk away unharmed once, but you're wrong. Those people are animals. They will hunt you down and…and…"

"Tie me to a lamppost and cut my head off," I said without emotion, and his eyes bulged. "Because I've seen them do that. Or maybe they'll brand me like a farm animal." I slid up the sleeve of my shirt and exposed the burn marks on my arm. "There are so many options, I don't know where to start."

His faced paled, and he looked like he might be sick. "Why the hell did you go back there? I can't believe you broke into the compound and put yourself in danger again."

"I didn't break into the compound. I was a guest." I shrugged as though I didn't have a care in the world. "In fact, one of them gave me all those documents. He even arranged my first meeting with a newspaper."

A wall of sadness punched me in the gut as the memory of my last moments with Ryker drifted to the forefront of my mind. As of yesterday, his phone was disconnected. I didn't know if he was alive or if I'd ever hear from him again. I scoured the internet searching for news on the Vargas Cartel daily. Fortunately or unfortunately, I didn't find a single article mentioning Ryker or Ignacio. I had no way to contact him. Noah disappeared two days ago. He left a scrap of paper on the kitchen counter with his cell phone number. I could call him, but the way our last conversation went, I promised myself I'd only contact him as a last resort.

"You're collaborating with the Vargas Cartel," my dad said, sounding lost and confused.

"I guess so."

"Why would you do that? Why would you put yourself in danger like that?"

"I didn't have a choice. Senator Deveron paid the Vargas Cartel to abduct me. Nobody would believe me unless I provided evidence to support my allegation."

"So you went to a criminal organization for help?"

"I didn't have any other options. Besides, I wasn't scared."

My phone vibrated on the coffee table. I didn't recognize the number, so I pressed ignore and slipped it into my pocket.

"I'm the US Attorney General. Of course you had options. You could've talked to your parents."

I scoffed. "I tried that. Mom ignored everything I said."

My dad winced. "I know, but if you'd given us some time, we would've come around."

"Yeah, and in the meantime, Mom would've continued to shove Evan down my throat."

"You didn't give us much time to come to terms

201

with the accusations. You disappeared a few days later," my dad said, dropping his voice an octave. "We didn't know what to believe. You were acting erratically."

"It all worked out," I said as I walked toward the hallway. "Now if you'll excuse me, I have some stuff to take care of before I leave."

The light shuffle of my dad's sneakers followed me down the hall and into Ryker's bedroom. Without looking at him, I sorted through the stacks of clothes on the bed next to my open suitcase. I'd gone shopping earlier in the day to buy more clothes. Most of my things were still at Vera's house and wearing the same five outfits had lost its appeal a week ago.

"Are you going somewhere?" my dad asked, leaning his shoulder against the espresso stained doorjamb.

"I'm thinking about it." I counted the number of shirts and then placed them at the bottom of the suitcase.

"Were you going to tell us or did you plan to disappear again?"

I whirled around, my hands raised in the air. "Why would I tell you or Mom anything? You're always busy with work. You barely have a minute to spare for me. Mom only wants me in her life when I'm her puppet doing whatever she wants."

"That's not entirely true," he whispered, his voice raw, pleading with me to understand.

I cocked my hip to the side. "You and mom spent all of an hour with me the day Evan brought me home from Mexico. You were both counting the minutes until you could run away. I felt like you couldn't stand to look at me. Like I had simultaneously disappointed and inconvenienced you."

He licked his lips. "I'm sorry if you felt that way. We didn't know what to do. We didn't know what to say. There isn't a textbook on how to handle what happened to you."

Closing my eyes momentarily, I sucked a deep breath into my lungs. "You could've acted like I mattered. Like you were happy I was home. Like you loved me." I tugged on the ends of my hair. "Jesus, Dad, it's not rocket science."

"You do matter," he said almost soundlessly. "We love you. I'm sorry if we failed to show you how much."

"Great, well, now you don't need to worry about it," I said, turning back around.

"What's that supposed to mean?"

I shrugged my shoulders. "It means that if you want me in your life, you need to support me and trust my decisions."

"We can do that."

I placed another stack of clothes in the suitcase. "All right." My phone vibrated again. It was the same number. My heart raced thinking it could be Ryker. "I need to take this."

"Okay." He scrubbed a hand down the side of his face. "Will you call me later? I'm not done talking to you."

"Yes."

"Thanks." He kissed me on the cheek. "Don't give up on your mom and me yet. We aren't perfect parents, but we love you."

I nodded. "I won't."

"Hello," I said as I heard the front door close.

"Hattie?"

My heart rocketed at the sound of his roughened voice. "Ryker. I've been insanely worried about you. Where are you? Why is your phone disconnected? What's going on? Did you see the news about Senator Deveron?"

He chuckled, and the deep laugh danced down my spine like a lover's caress. "Slow down."

"Just tell me what going on," I demanded.

"I had to disconnect my phone for security reasons. This is the new number. Yes, I've seen the news and I'm still in Mexico."

"Oh." My shoulders drooped, and I inhaled shakily. A big part of me had hoped he was already in D.C. "I miss you."

"I miss you, too. How are you holding up? Are you feeling okay?"

"I'm a little nauseous on some mornings, but nothing too crazy."

"Good. How are things with your parents?" His voice was gruff.

"Not so good, but my dad wants things to change. He just left a few minutes ago."

"Did you work out everything with Ignacio?"

Ryker didn't say anything for a prolonged beat. "I'm still working on a few details."

I twisted my fingers into interwoven knots. "How much longer?" I couldn't take being separated from him for much longer. I was lonely.

"Strange you should bring that up," he said. I

could hear the smile in his voice, and a matching smile stretched across my face. I loved playful Ryker.

"Why's that?"

"Because there will be a private plane waiting for you at Ronald Reagan Washington National Airport at two in the afternoon tomorrow. Do you think you can find it in your heart to clear your schedule?"

"You're not playing with me right now, are you? Because I might reach through the phone and strangle you if this is a hoax."

He chuckled. "Good thing I'm absolutely serious."

I curled my free hand into the hem of my skirt. "I missed you. It feels like it's been months instead of weeks since I've talked to you."

"I know. I wanted to call you every single day, but I couldn't. I had to make Ignacio and Emanuel think I was done with you."

"I realize that, but it didn't make it any easier." I slipped the elastic band out of my hair and leaned back on the bed. "Are you sure it's safe for me to come?"

"Of course, I wouldn't have arranged a flight for you if it weren't."

My brows knitted together. "But you said you were still working out some details," I pointed out.

"I am, but it's nothing that you need to worry about."

I nodded before realizing he couldn't see me. "Okay."

"Can I expect you to get on that plane

tomorrow?"

I smiled, the tension in my chest easing for the first time in weeks. "It shouldn't be a problem. I'm already packed."

"Why'd you do that?"

I propped my hand behind my head as I chewed on my lower lip. "If I didn't hear from you in the next day or two I planned to go find you."

"Hmm. Good to know." I heard a hushed male voice in the background. "Hold on a second," he said. I heard his phone brush against his hand, muffling the conversation.

I tapped my finger on my thigh waiting for him to talk to me again. Seconds felt like hours. I stared at the empty white walls of his apartment. I listened to the faint hum of the air conditioning unit. Then, he was back.

He sighed. "I have to go. I need to take care of a few things."

"Oh," I said, sitting up. My mood shifted and suddenly I felt melancholy. "I guess I'll see you tomorrow, then."

"Tomorrow," he said softly.

"Sounds good," I replied instead of saying goodbye because I wasn't ready to sever the connection yet. I wanted to squeeze as many words as I could out of him.

"I'm sorry. I wish I had more time to talk. I miss hearing your voice and talking to you whenever I want."

"I understand." My voice wobbled.

"Hey, don't get all sad on me. I don't have anything planned after I pick you up at the airport except for spending every moment with you."

I smiled. "I love that."

"I love you," he responded.

A shivered ran through me and my smile came back. "I love you, too."

Chapter Twenty~Seven

Hattie

A salty breezed shuffled through my hair as I paused at the bottom of the stairs of the private jet. I scanned the area, looking for Ryker. A smile split across my face the instant I spotted him. He was leaning up against the wall with his legs spread, and his hands stuffed deep in the pockets of his linen pants. The top two buttons of his gray polo shirt were open, his eyes trained on me.

I broke into a sprint, my turquoise ballet flats slapping against the asphalt, the wheels of my luggage bellowing protest. I halted about a foot away from him, suddenly feeling shy. My eyes trailed down his wide chest to his narrow waist and back up again.

"Come here," he said, crooking his finger at me, his lids heavy.

I closed the distance between us and his strong hands immediately circled my hips, pulling me flush against his body. I could feel the heat radiating from his body right through my clothes.

"Hi," I whispered.

"Hi," he said, a lopsided smile on his heavenly lips.

I brushed his smooth jaw with the pads of my fingertips and my skin tingled. "I can't believe I'm finally here. It seemed like I'd never find my way back to you."

Tenderness washed over his face, and his eyes crinkled at the corners, softening ever so slightly. Like magic, I swayed into him, burying my head in the crook of his neck. His familiar scent filled my lungs and I smiled like a kid on Christmas morning.

"The car is waiting for us. Are you ready to go?"

I dragged my hands up his chest. "When are we going to the Vargas compound?"

He framed my jaw with his hands, tilting up my face. "Tomorrow."

"Where are going now?"

He kissed the corner of mouth. "It's a surprise."

I narrowed my eyes, but I couldn't erase the smile on my face. I was too happy. "What kind of surprise? It better be good."

"I think it is, but you'll have to let me know what you think," he said, his eyes twinkling.

"I'll do that."

He stared at me for a second, then he brushed his hand down my face. "How's the baby?"

I slid his hand from my hip to my belly. "I think I'm showing a little."

"Maybe a little." He pressed a soft kiss on my temple. "We need to find you a doctor."

I nodded. "Tomorrow."

Grabbing my suitcase from me, he threaded his

fingers through mine and pulled me toward a black SUV with dark tinted windows.

***

An hour later, we stopped in front of a large white stucco bungalow with a thatched roof. It sat on a nearly deserted stretch of white sandy beach bordered by the clearest blue water I'd ever seen. Orange and pink brushstrokes painted the sky where it met the ocean. A few boats dotted the horizon, but other than that, it looked like our private paradise.

"What do you think?" Ryker said as he opened my door.

"It's beautiful." I climbed out of the passenger seat and tilted my head to the side. The faint roar of the ocean mixed with the soft swish of the trees swaying in the wind brought a smile to my face.

"You're not disappointed. We can go somewhere—"

"I love it," I cut in, then I shook my head. "What is this place? How'd you find it?"

"Somebody gave it to Ignacio a couple of years ago in exchange for a debt. He has never used it."

"He doesn't care that we're here?"

He slipped his fingers through mine. "He doesn't have a choice."

I cocked an eyebrow. "Do you want to explain?"

"Not today. I want today to be about us."

I hesitated for a second, not sure what to say. He'd hid the truth from me in the past. I didn't like being in the dark. It made me nervous. "Ryker," I said, drawing out his name. "Don't keep secrets from me."

"There's nothing to worry about. I promise."

His phone buzzed, and he glanced at the screen. "You're not hungry, are you?"

"No, I ate more than enough on the plane, but I think you already know that since you arranged the whole thing."

"Then, let's catch the last few minutes of the *puesta de sol*."

"The what?" I said.

"The sunset." He smiled at me as he guided us through the house and to the patio overlooking the ocean. "One of these days, I'm going to teach you Spanish."

"Maybe," I said noncommittally as I gazed at the beauty in front of me.

The palm trees lining the sides of the patio swayed in the gentle tropical breeze. Tiny white lights zigzagged from tree to tree. A small round table complete with a white tablecloth and three flickering candles in different sizes was positioned in the middle of the patio.

"This is amazing," I whispered.

Ryker pulled out my chair, and I sat down. "I'm glad you like it. I was a little worried the traffic would make us miss the sunset, but it all worked out," he said, waving his hand in the direction of the setting sun.

"Yes, it did. How'd you do all this?"

He poured two glasses of champagne from the open bottle in an ice bucket and handed me one. "Rever helped."

Dumbfounded, I shook my head. "How'd that

happen? I thought he left the country with Anna."

Ryker's lips tightened. "That didn't work out so well."

"What happened?"

He sighed. "Long story. She lied about everything. About being pregnant. Her continued involvement with the Alvarez Cartel. Her feelings for Rever."

I glanced to the side. "I'm sorry," I said, not sure what to say.

"It worked out. Rever and I are in a better place now, and he's already over it." He held up his glass. "To new beginnings."

"To us," I said, tapping my glass against his. I took a sip and the tiny bubbles danced on my tongue. "I'm glad you and Rever worked things out."

He rubbed his finger along the rim of his glass. "Growing up, we were never close. I used to blame our problems on him, but in retrospect, I realize Ignacio pitted us against each other. He bragged about all of my successes to Rever, and he constantly reminded me that Rever was his only legitimate son and heir. I never stopped trying to prove I was smarter and braver than Rever." He shook his head. "I thought a long list of accomplishments would erase the error of my birth and make me worthy of my father's love and attention."

"How do you feel now?"

"I'm indifferent. I don't care what he thinks anymore. He's not perfect, but you know what I do care about?" He tugged on my sleeve.

"What?"

He inched closer to me and his knee brushed against my bare thigh. A ribbon of heat shot up my leg. "That you've done a half of dozen things to avoid kissing me tonight. Should I be offended?"

Flames rolled up my face and my exhalation fractured. I planned to spend my life with Ryker. I suspected he knew me better than my parents and my friends, but I'd been unable to relax around him since he picked me up at the airport. Now that we'd overcome all the obstacles to our relationship, I was scared and more than a little nervous. The incongruity of my emotions didn't escape my attention.

I held up my thumb and index finger. "I'm a little bit nervous."

Grinning, he stared at me with his smoky eyes. "We'll have to change that," he said playfully.

My eyebrows lifted, and I leaned forward a couple of inches. "I'm curious. How do you plan to do that? Do you have a magic wand tucked in your pants somewhere?" A laugh burst from his mouth and for a blissful second I didn't understand what was so funny.

"As a matter of a fact, I think I do."

I shoved his shoulder when the innuendo registered in my brain. "Shut up. I didn't mean it that way."

He angled his head to the side. "No?"

"No," I said, unable to stop the smile from spreading across my face.

"That's too bad."

"Why's that?"

He tugged on my arms, sliding me onto his lap and my eyes flared. My breasts grazed his firm chest, and he splayed one hand over my lower back. The heat of his body burned right through me.

"I think you're on to something," he whispered next to my ear, his thumb tracing my collarbone.

Anticipation zipped through my nerve endings. "Really? How so?" I said breathlessly as I clutched the solid muscles of his shoulders.

His hand curled around the back of my neck, toying with the knot of my halter top. My heart hammered against by breastbone and my stomach coiled into a ball of longing. He leaned back and his eyes locked on mine with so much smoldering heat, my breath tripped in my lungs.

"If you're ready to go inside, I'd be happy to show you."

"I thought you'd never ask," I choked out, my chest aching with love for him.

He rose out of the chair, and I wrapped my legs around his waist. Almost immediately, his mouth found mine. I closed my eyes, and I released all the fears and anxiety plaguing me. This night was about reclaiming our future, and I'd be damned if I would waste it tying myself into knots, worrying about things I couldn't control.

He laid me down on a platform bed covered with white rose petals. White gauzy material hung from the ceiling in billowing waves. Candles lined the mahogany nightstands. Shadows from the flickering flames danced on the creamy walls. The ocean scent from the open patio doors filled the air.

"This is beautiful. I love it."

He kneeled on the bed and brushed his fingertips down my cheek. The light touch sent shivers down my spine. "You're beautiful."

Caught in his gaze, words escaped me, but it didn't matter. In a flash, his lips swept over mine in a soul-searching kiss. A languid heat flowed through my limbs as his lips made their way down my body. In a haze, I barely noticed the clothes disappearing from my body one item at a time. His hands and his lips touched every inch of my skin, teasing me, loving me, and worshipping me until I thought I'd spontaneously combust.

"Too slow," I whispered without opening my eyes.

I felt his lips curve into a smile against my neck. "I want to show you how much I love you."

"By teasing my body until I die?"

The deep rumble of his chuckle sent goosebumps tumbling down my arms. "Is that what I'm doing?"

"Yes." I grabbed the hem of his shirt and yanked it over his head.

"You're so impatient."

"I want to feel and touch you too." I kissed the hollow of his neck as I unbuttoned his pants and shoved them along with his boxer briefs down his legs.

He groaned softly. "Okay. You win. I can't resist you. You know that, right?"

I wrapped my arms around his waist. His skin felt so smooth and toned beneath my fingertips. "I'll keep that in mind in the future."

He traced a line from my knee to the inside of my thigh just inches from my aching center. He drew lazy circles with the pads of his fingers, and I struggled to catch my breath.

"Touch me," I moaned.

I gasped as he slid one finger inside of me. His finger moved in and out as his thumb rubbed maddening circles around my clit.

"Like this? Is this what you want?" His voice was husky with desire.

"Yes. No. Yes. No," I mumbled, my hips bucking of their own volition, already greedy for more.

"No?" He chuckled again as he spread my legs wider and braced his hands next to my head. In one smooth motion, he shifted his body above me, teasing me with the feel of his hard length as it grazed my sex.

"Yes," I moaned as he trailed wet kisses down my neck. Seconds from unraveling, I wrapped my legs around the backs of his thighs, locking my ankles together. "I need you."

His hand cupped my backside, and he pushed inside of me. The sensation of being stretched and filled by him felt like it lasted for an eternity. For a few beats, he didn't move as if he were too busy savoring the feeling of being connected again. Then, it started. His first few strokes were slow and gentle. The ocean breeze swept up my needy moans and carried them out to sea.

"I never want to leave this bed," he said against my mouth, his hips rolling in sync with mine.

"Neither do I," I whispered, meaning every word I said.

Then, his hand circled my waist, driving into me

harder and faster until we were both lost in the moment.

Lost in the passion.

Lost in the pleasure.

Lost in each other.

With my head buried next to his shoulder, I clung to the roped muscles hugging his spine as our hips moved against each other. It was as though the last three weeks of uncertainty and darkness hadn't happened. Everything was light again. The rightness of being with Ryker made my heart swell and my head spin. I loved this man.

As the thought registered in my mind, my release rushed through me fast, hard and unexpected. Cries of pleasure somersaulted from my mouth one after another as a million nerve endings burst into flame inside of me. Two hard thrusts and Ryker followed me over the edge.

For long seconds, he buried his head in the crook of my neck, slowly rocking in and out of me. Time stood still. I never wanted it to end and for the first time since I met him, I believed it didn't have to.

"What's the date?" he murmured, not lifting his head.

"The fifteenth. Why?"

He pressed a kiss against my lips. "Because I never want to forget the day we started our lives together."

Chapter Twenty-Eight

Ryker

Hattie, Rever and I stood on the tarmac next to the airstairs, leading to Ignacio's private jet. Ignacio stared through us like we were invisible.

He handed his small carry-on bag to Noah. "Give me a minute," Ignacio said.

After we had revealed Emanuel's deception, we told Ignacio it was time for him to retire. He screamed at us. He threatened us, but in the end he agreed. I think he knew it was time to hand over the reins of the Vargas Cartel. He had some lingering health problems from being shot in the chest and Emanuel's deception made him look weak.

Noah met my gaze, and I nodded. "It's fine. He's not going anywhere." I'd hired Noah to escort Ignacio out of Mexico. Unlike the other people affiliated with the Vargas Cartel, he didn't harbor any feelings of loyalty toward Ignacio.

Ignacio stared at his feet for a minute, then trained his dark eyes on me. "You know, I'd always hoped that my sons would take their place in the

Vargas Cartel."

Hattie squeezed my hand, showing her support without words.

"I know," I conceded. "You didn't exactly keep it secret."

Ignacio pursed his lips and shoved his hands into his pockets. "I guess not."

Rever grinned and slapped Ignacio on the arm. "Looks like you got your wish."

Ignacio scoffed. "I'd never dreamed my sons would push me out to make it happen."

"Senator Deveron and his son were indicted last week," I pointed out. "It's only a matter of time before the US government requests your extradition for cocaine smuggling, money laundering and a long list of other shit the Deverons feed them."

Ignacio shrugged. "It'll never happen."

"Either way, it's time for new leadership," I reiterated for the hundredth time in the last week. Ignacio believed the Mexican government wouldn't approve his request for extradition because he had too much evidence implicating high-level government officials. He was probably right. Even if the Mexican government imprisoned Ignacio, they'd orchestrate his escape from prison and subsequent disappearance like so many other powerful drug lords before him.

"That's what you say now, but don't be too stubborn to call me when things fall apart. I'm not too proud to come back and help my sons."

Rever rolled his eyes. "Don't worry. We'll be just fine."

"I doubt it."

"You don't know when to shut up, do you?" Rever snarled.

"I successfully managed the business for almost two decades. That's unheard of in the world of drug cartels. You need my guidance."

"Guess what?" Rever said. "You didn't do such a good job. Emanuel nearly stole the whole thing from you while you were busy meddling in our lives."

"I would've figured it out with or without you two," Ignacio snarled.

"You know," Rever hissed. "I'm done with this shit. Ryker, I'll meet you in the car." He turned on his heel and left.

Hattie leaned into me, pressing her lips against my cheek. "I'll go talk to him."

I turned to watch her until she was safely ensconced in the car. I had a hard time leaving her alone. I felt like she could be snatched away at any second.

"I give this six months," Ignacio said.

I turned to face him. "What?"

"You and Ryker trying to run my cartel."

"Why's that?" I asked, but immediately regretting it.

"You're too soft and Rever's a hothead. Rever will kill indiscriminately, and you'll spend all your time cleaning up his messes and apologizing for his behavior." A bitter laugh tumbled from his mouth. "I'm almost sorry I won't be around to watch it happen."

I pinched the bridge of my nose. Unlike Rever, I refused to be baited. Ignacio had been lashing out at us for days. The insults made Rever crazy, but I understood what Ignacio was doing. He wanted us to change our minds and let him stay.

"We'll see."

Ignacio gripped the metal tube stair railing. "Yeah, well, I better get going before that asshole you hired drags me up the stairs."

"Love you, Dad," I said when he reached the top of the stairs.

He paused, his entire body tensing. "I know." He glanced over his shoulder. "I love you, too. I love both of my sons. I just wish you'd let me be in your life."

I smiled even as my heart constricted. "Maybe someday."

He rubbed a wrinkled hand along the side of his face. "Goodbye, Ryker."

"Goodbye, Dad," I whispered.

Epilogue

Hattie

I dug my toes into the pristine white sand and the waves crashed around my ankles. I lifted my chin, letting my head hang back, drinking up the sun. A few wispy white clouds dotted the blue sky. A seagull swooped and cawed as it dove into the turquoise water. It was a perfect day.

Three years had passed since Ryker and I officially started our lives together at this beach bungalow. While there had been moments of uncertainty, particularly in the first year, our life together exceeded my wildest dreams.

Almost two and half years ago, I married Ryker in a small, private ceremony on this beach with only Rever and my best friend, Vera, in attendance. When I asked Vera to be my maid of honor, she cried. Without confronting her, she confessed she'd sent emails to Evan informing him of my whereabouts after we broke up. Apparently, she wanted to show him I had moved on. Once she learned about Senator Deveron's connection to the

Vargas Cartel and his role in my abduction, she said the guilt nearly killed her. She told me she thought she had lost her best friend. I promised her she hadn't.

I didn't see her as much as I would've liked over the last few years because Ryker and I floated between Mexico, the US, and his flat in London. Our son, Easton, was almost three years old, so we figured we had a few more years of traveling before we had to commit to living in one place.

My parents didn't accept Ryker in the beginning, particularly after they discovered his connection to the Vargas Cartel, but their opposition had softened after Easton was born. My relationship with them was complicated, and I didn't think it would change anytime in the near future. They hadn't pushed me out of their life, and for that I was thankful. Easton needed as much family as he could get.

I hadn't seen or heard from Ignacio since that day on the tarmac, but I didn't mind. Ryker never indicated whether he kept in contact with him, and I didn't think I'd ever ask. Ryker's mom spent a month with us after Easton was born, but she claimed she'd met the love of her life. She'd moved to some undisclosed location, and we only saw her once a year. When I asked Ryker if he cared, he just shrugged, claiming he was happy his mom had found someone after spending most of her life alone. Something told me Ignacio had rekindled things with Ryker's mom, but when I asked him about, Ryker just smiled and changed the subject.

Rever was a surprisingly gentle uncle, but we only saw him a handful of times a year. Ryker and

Rever ran the Vargas Cartel together for the first six months after they forced Ignacio out. Fortunately, Rever quickly proved he was more than capable of running everything alone, and Ryker bowed out. I suspected Ryker still managed the books, but he never confirmed it. I think it was his way of keeping Easton and me as far away from the violence as possible.

I finally finished my master's degree last year and after turning down several job offers, I started writing a book exposing how criminal organizations have infiltrated governments throughout history. I didn't know if I'd ever do anything with it, but it kept me busy.

A light, tinkling giggle floated through the air as Ryker's arms closed around my waist, and two tiny hands wrapped around my leg.

"Found you, Mommy," Easton said.

I gazed down at Easton's gray eyes so much like Ryker's and my breath caught in my throat. He and Ryker were proof the most amazing things could come from hardship. "I guess this wasn't a very good hiding place."

Ryker spun me around to face him. His fingers trailed down my cheek, and his lips tugged down at the corners. "Coming back here this weekend was your idea. Why are you crying?" he asked, studying me with quiet concern.

I smiled through my tears. "Because our life is perfect."

His lips curled up into a smile, his eyes gleaming with mischief. "After everything we went through to get here, don't you think we earned it?"

"Yes." I scooped Easton up and plopped him on my hip. "I think it's time for your nap, little man."

Ryker wrapped his arm around my shoulders, and we strolled over the hot sand back into the beach bungalow.

Easton rubbed his eyes. "I'm not tired. I want to play."

"You have to sleep."

"Why?" Easton asked, his lower lip puffing out in a practiced pout.

Ryker snatched Easton out of my arms and placed him in the middle of his bed. "You need to rest because when you wake up we're all going to build the biggest sand castle ever." Ryker pulled the covers over Easton body.

"So you need to sleep too?"

"Yes." Ryker kissed Easton's forehead. "Mommy and Daddy are going to take a big nap, too."

I raised one eyebrow. "Really?"

He smirked as he threaded his hand through mine and pulled me out the door. "Yeah, I have to show you something."

"Something important?"

"I'd like to think it's important, but I'll wait for your confirmation."

"Hmm," I said. "The magic wand in your pants?"

"Exactly." He tipped his head back and laughed. "Only you would remember that."

"Only you would twist my words like that," I countered.

He lifted me up and swung me over his shoulder.

"Hey! Don't manhandle me."

"You like it when I manhandle you," he said, spanking me lightly on the backs of my thighs.

"You wish," I said, laughing as he dropped me on the bed.

Grinning, he stretched his body out over mine. I ran my hands over his sculpted tan chest. "No, you're wrong," he whispered as his lips brushed against mine. "All of my wishes came true the minute you said 'I do.' I have a perfect wife, a perfect son, and the perfect life. I don't need anything else."

I cupped his chin and placed one of his hands on my lower stomach. "Are you sure about that?"

"Yes," he murmured as he feathered kisses down my neck.

Ribbons of heat raced down my body, and I arched my hips. "That's too bad," I rasped out, my voice already thick with desire.

"Why's that?" he asked as he untied the top of my bikini.

"Because I'm pregnant." We'd been trying for over a year. Just last month, Ryker and I decided to let fate take its course. If it didn't happen, it wasn't meant to be.

He lifted his gaze, and his eyes locked on mine, his smile widening. "Seriously?"

I nodded. "Seriously."

"Hattie." He laid his hand tenderly against my cheek. "Do you know how happy you make me?"

"Show me."

And he did exactly that.

Acknowledgements

Some books are easier to write than others. I wanted to give Hattie and Ryker's story the right ending. I went back and forth, rethinking my plans for the story so many times. I never thought I'd finish the third book. I hope it didn't disappoint.

Thanks to Limitless Publishing for supporting me and being available to answer all my questions. You make everything easy.

Thanks to Rosa Sophia for combing over this book with great attention to detail.

Thanks to Shannon Hunt for coordinating the cover reveal and release.

Thanks to my husband for reading this and cleaning up my dialogue.

Thanks to all the readers and bloggers. I appreciate all of your messages, reviews, and words of encouragement.

About the Author

After spending years practicing law and a million other things, Lisa decided to pursue her dream of becoming a writer and she must confess that inventing characters is so much more fun than writing contracts and legal briefs. A native of Colorado, she lives with her husband and three children in Denver.

Facebook:
https://www.facebook.com/lcardiff11

Twitter:
https://twitter.com/lcardiff_author

Website:
http://lisacardiff.com/

Goodreads:
https://www.goodreads.com/author/show/7692079.
Lisa_Cardiff